BRANWELL

Born in Virginia in 1973, Douglas A. Martin was raised in Georgia and, in 1998, moved to New York, where he has taught writing at the New School University since 2001. He has published three books of poetry: *my gradual demise & honeysuckle*, *Servicing the Salamander*, and *the haiku year* (co-author). His first novel, *Outline of My Lover*, has been adapted by the Ballett Frankfurt (now the Bill Forsythe Company) for their multimedia production Kammer/Kammer, which they have performed all over the world. His story collection, *They Change the Subject*, has also recently been published.

ABOUT THIS BOOK

"Martin avoids the temptation of plunging headfirst into the gothic, instead conveying Branwell's psychic turmoil in simple, stripped-down sentences... [He] sparsely fills in the outlines of Branwell's dissolution, a suitably phantom account of the man who painted himself out of his own family portrait." *Village Voice*

"[A] moving and evocative portrait of a boy doomed to enter history as a sad footnote to his sisters' lives... it invites the reader to join Douglas Martin in his dream of Branwell Brontë—a dream so enchantingly and hypnotically rendered that the invitation is a pleasure to accept." *The Brooklyn Rail*

"[A] lyrical study of human nature and the destructive power of potential. With Hemingway-sized spatters of histrionic prose, author Douglas Martin vividly paints the mad landscape of childhood imagination." *Baltimore City Paper*

"[C]onsistently heartbreaking and provocative... Martin's poignant, third person narrative of Branwell's lives also gives us finely detailed glimpses of the more familiar Brontës. Charlotte's stern, disapproving older sister persona, Emily's brooding but loving presence, and Ann's quiet, pensive, spiritual strength are juxtaposed to Branwell's tragic romanticism." *Small Spiral Notebook*

"[S]tylistically complex and emotionally evocative. Branwell Brontë emerges as a fascinating lost character, both muse and devil to his sisters' passions, giving us a new dimension to this ever fascinating family." Darcy Steinke

"[L]yrical, hypnotic, genre-bending. Martin's novel functions as a fictional essay on the troubled, alluring legend of Branwell Brontë, as well as a truly poetic experiment in how to push autobiographical fantasy to its limits. I enjoyed it immensely." Wayne Koestenbaum

"A tender, tragic portrayal of a doomed artist... This volume's beautiful declarative sentences are perfectly fitted to this famously imaginative, headstrong family; they bring Branwell Brontë's world to light." *Publishers Weekly*

DOUGLAS A. MARTIN

BRANWELL

A NOVEL

A Brandon Original Paperback

First published in Britain and Ireland in 2007 by
Brandon
an imprint of Mount Eagle Publications
Dingle, Co. Kerry, Ireland and
Unit 3, Olympia Trading Estate, Coburg Road,
London N22 6TZ, England

www.brandonbooks.com

2 4 6 8 10 9 7 5 3 1

Copyright © Douglas A. Martin 2006

The right of Douglas A. Martin to be identified as Author of this Work has been asserted
by him in accordance with the Copyright, Designs and Patents Act 1988.

Brandon/Mount Eagle Publications receives support from
the Arts Council/An Chomhairle Ealaíon.

First published in North America by Soft Skull Press, New York.

ISBN 978-0-86322-363-1

Cover design: Design Suite
Typesetting by Red Barn Publishing, Skeagh, Skibbereen
Printed in the UK

This book is dedicated to my sister, who wrote poetry as a girl, and Ms. Havrilla, who first taught me Emily.

When my children were very young, when, as far as I can remember, the oldest was about ten years of age, and the youngest about four, thinking that they knew more than I had yet discovered, in order to make them speak with less timidity, I deemed that if they were put under a sort of cover, I might gain my end.

—Patrick Brontë

THEIR BROTHER IS BORN not long after Charlotte. The only son, he is given both the father's and the mother's names. Patrick Branwell Brontë. Their son is the gift they've been praying for. He is three when the family moves from Thorton to Haworth. Their father has been appointed to the church there.

The parsonage is the last and highest house in the village, beyond the wall of the church, two stories of gray stone, the roof slate. The floors are stone. Only two rooms will ever be carpeted. Their father, in his fear of fire, does not want to put up any curtains over the windows.

Seven windows look outside from the front of the house, holding their family of eight. Maria, Elizabeth, Charlotte, he, Emily, Anne, and their mother, Maria Branwell, their father, Patrick Brontë.

Within the family, because of his sex, he is afforded a special place, privileged. They will try to give him a certain status, as their real achievement. He is an ardent boy, their father's son who will prove to be so mercurial.

Childhood was Branwell's kingdom to rule over.

Their father wanted his children dressed in wool and silk. Cotton and flannel would burn too quickly, if they caught fire. The walls were lime-washed. Sheep came right up to the house to graze, and the rooms upstairs overlooked the graves of the churchyard. From the kitchen you could see, at the back of the house, moors.

Their mother's health was failing, after the first, after the second, after the third child, then Branwell, then Emily. Anne is born on a day the rest of the children would have to spend with neighbors.

Their aunt, their mother's sister, had come to help give a hand. She'd visited the day their little son was born, too. Six children now to look after, and their mother was spending more and more time in bed.

After tea, she would try to come downstairs to play with the boy, Branwell.

It was twilight. He was four.

Their mother playing with him in the evening in the parlor, that was the only thing Charlotte would remember of their mother, who will die.

Maria is the one who will teach him and Charlotte to read and count. It is Maria who will take him into her bed, late at night, when he is having a nightmare.

She sings him back to sleep.

The world seems to float by his eyes when she holds him in her arms, when she rocks him that way. Or she takes him outside to play, holding his hand pointing out to show him around.

Deep tenderness for him comes as a feeling of pain in the chest.

She holds him like she holds her breath.

He is her favorite, so he'll pay the most visits to the sickroom.

When they go to school, the girls will then know they never really learned Grammar, never really knew Geography, that they were lacking in so many other things they didn't yet know.

The schools used to be mills, warehouses. Heaps of lime stain the fields.

But Branwell would remain home. Their father didn't want to let him out of his sights. He was not to be tested yet. And Anne was still at home, too. Anne was still too young to go off to school. Though she wanted to walk out and about with everyone else, just like everyone else.

At Cowan Bridge the girls were all to learn History, How to Use a Globe, Arithmetic, Needlework, of course, Housework, How to Tend to Fine Linens, perhaps some French. Each girl was to have with her her Bible when she arrived, her prayer book, her workbag full of sewing implements, gloves, patterns.

Maria and Elizabeth and Charlotte were off at school, and Emily was soon to follow. She'd been registered by their father for the school. He had to do something with all the children.

Then his daughter Maria was sent home ill. Branwell could spend more time with her. She was the first he was to love on earth, the first body he knew. She'd held him, recognizing his fragility. She'd bent down over him in bed to gently kiss the top of his head, to bless him And then his sister Maria, like their mother Maria Branwell, had died.

*

They'd awoken to church bells. The parish was right outside their window. A whole world was held inside that the bells would draw their mother out of. She had suffered a galloping cancer, aggravated by consumption.

Before he knew words, he'd known speech simply as this music, the music of Maria. His mother, his sister. He'd remember the name again in poems.

She'd had a soul. At an early age, he'd known that. Maria had tried her hardest then to comfort those their mother had brought into the world. For them, Christmas would always be associated with her, that sister who'd become like the mother they knew only as the smallest of children. Sometimes it confused them in their memories, this Maria and Maria.

At home, in memory of her, they begin calling him Branwell, now that their mother has died. To call him this is also to distinguish him from his father.

His father wants to try to take the boy's mind off all these things he goes silent under. For one Christmas, the boy is given soldiers. To supplement the soldiers his father has given him, he'll get a set of Turkish musicians, from a store in Halifax. Halifax is within walking distance. He's been admiring the soldiers, the musicians, all in the window. There is just a little bit of money to spend, but his father wants to get the set for his son. And one day they'll buy a whole box of Indians. Branwell tries to recreate the Battle of Washington, while his father practices his sermon in the other room.

They can hear him all over the house.

Charlotte wants to play, too.

I will go to war with you, little Branwell.

*

Not long after his mother Maria and his sister Maria died, Elizabeth had also been brought home from the school where all his sisters were sent. The whooping cough, measles, these things had descended on them. And they didn't get better. It was the school their father had sent them all off to. But not his son. Never him. He wouldn't be sent off.

He was playing with his soldiers on the carpet, while Elizabeth was sick, too, while Elizabeth was dying, too. Over and over again in his mind they died. Maria, Maria. Maria was dying again.

Then their father wanted all of them back home, all of them. Charlotte and Emily returned just in time, just before Elizabeth died, a month or so only after the smartest, Maria. Elizabeth, the third to go since their coming to the parsonage at Haworth. They'd only been there five years. Only Charlotte, Emily, and Anne were left now. And he. They would spend the next six years all home together with their father, all of the family, there together, Charlotte oldest.

Even without those deaths early in his life, their brother might have become the person he would, might have always carried a fearful temperament inside him. Maria was the one he couldn't seem to forget. He remembered his father had brought her home from school, from Cowan Bridge, where they were supposed to grow into good girls. She'd stayed in bed all day, in the sick room, the room his aunt, Miss Branwell, would use when she came to stay with them. Maria talked about the wonderful journey she was about to take, in dying.

They felt gravity now, that's what it meant.

His aunt wanted him to come see his sister in her coffin.

Living across from the dark, old church, they'd be reminded of more deaths every day, their own feeling already imminent.

Church bells meant there was about to be a funeral.

They'd dressed for Maria all in black, the house sunny and silent but for bells.

She had taught him to say his prayers, had been like a mother to him.

He would have been about eight.

He'd clung to her.

She'd had a saintlike aspect, a complete belief in the mercy of God above.

He hears do not grieve.

If they're good, they'll see her again one day.

She is gone, her body removed from the house. Her smile in death stays in his mind. He holds onto her, inside. She'll never move again. Her hair must have been golden. There was sun on her cheeks. He's scared of the scene of separation. They lower her down into the earth. It's been opened up to take her inside. She will live down there now, under them, the parsonage forever home. She was their mother, their little mother, after her first death. The water from the yard collects and drains down to their well.

Now their aunt, their mother's sister, has to come look after them. Their father is a busy man, with the church. He will try to marry again, but the women he asks won't marry him. There's a friend of the family from Thornton he could ask, but she won't have him. A woman he loves won't marry him. A friendly but decisive no. And then there's a girl from an earlier parish, from his very first curacy, whom he had once thought he could do better than. She won't have him now.

He briefly considered asking the neighbor to accept his hand in marriage, the woman next door, where his children had often visited, but nothing comes of this passing thought.

Their aunt would just have to come and stay with them, to help raise them. It was her duty as the children's mother's sister. Miss Branwell, who'd been there already to nurse her sister and help with the burial, she'd never marry. She'd stay. She'd find the boy endearingly Irish, handsome, auburn-haired.

A man all alone like that, she'd have to help Mr. Brontë. There was the church to worry about, sermons to write, his duty as a man called to their God. The children scurried around like mice, with their mother dead.

*

It was Jesus who'd called away the mother of the Brontë children, and then Maria, and then Elizabeth. The boy has been told this, but he doesn't understand. He wants their father to explain better.

Tell him why Jesus was upset with them.

What have they done that was so bad.

They must have done something.

And if he's taken Maria, what is going to happen to him. What is he going to do to them.

For seven months she suffered, waiting only for Jesus to take her. She walked with him and his sisters, but her holiness had been envied by their great enemy, their father tells the boy, and it was this enemy that disturbed her mind through her last great conflict, causing her to suffer so.

Charlotte took her brother's hand, to leave their father alone now.

They began their writing when Charlotte was ten, Branwell nine, Emily eight, Anne six. Charlotte and her brother would work together as partners, while Emily and Anne continued to play together, even if what they were writing were called poems. They were beginning to construct another space, within which other people could live, have adventures and love.

The characters had to be strong enough to be believable, for the reader to feel they'd been brought to life.

Us two, that's what Charlotte says of Branwell and herself.

There's an Infernal World, there below them. That's what they'll call it. They can enter it in writing. They are never to forget that.

In the Parsonage, home, they are all safe.

Or outside, on the moors, as long as they all walk together, as long as they stay close to each other.

How did they ever think they could live without this place.

When Maria had died, she'd taken a part of them away with her. That which didn't fit into the greater scheme of life was killed. They had to know that. But death itself, it might be the greater scheme.

He'd write a poem for her called Caroline.

Maria was the first one of his sisters to leave him, named after their mother, after Maria, the first one of them to leave; but the rest of them could never leave each other or Haworth.

That's true.

Just he and Anne had been there when she'd died. Charlotte and Emily, they'd been off at school.

At this young age, already, outside, in wars, in the village, among others, there's a brutality that dominates and that they know. All those people in the village, their father just hadn't reached them yet.

As children, they'd all absorbed their father's Irish accent. The rhymes, the rhythms, of their childhood poems were dependent on this. Legends pass on this way. His father and Branwell walk into town, into the village, for the Leeds Intelligencer newspaper.

In the village was where they all talked funny.

Once they got back home, Branwell could read from the paper to them. Maria had taught him. His father was overprotective, and he'd also absolve him of all responsibility. His son was to be left alone, to develop in the way a boy should, falling back on his own judgment. He had hopes and plans for his only son. Branwell was to be the pride and joy of them all.

A great Irish hope. He'd make their fortune, for all of them, his father and his sisters. He'd have to be an artist, of some sort, be able to draw; or he'd have to be able to write. Already he was practicing with Charlotte. He is insecure, but he needs to be able to feel a certain power in something. There must be something he can control. He's to be granted certain privileges, as the only son. He's to be recognized as useful, as valuable.

He'd write a character for himself. His character would be tall, much taller than he is now. And his sisters would recognize him as dashing. He'd have personal freedom, his own, a way to escape, to escape from them all.

He'd be a pirate, an officer, a leader of the bandits. His excesses would be taken where he could get them. And even

21

his enemies would have to respect him. Even in their childhood games, in their childhood writings, the plays of stories they practice by telling each other, there were these enemies. There had to be. Only his family would still always love him, still always own him.

He had his set of toy soldiers, and they'd each pick out one to be. It's not like he could keep them away from his sisters, even if he had wanted to; but he gives one to each of them. Branwell is sharing. He has to.

They call his temperament Irish.

He's small in stature.

He has red hair, so he must be Irish, they all think in the village.

He'd rove here and there, according to his fancy, over the moors. He's a boy, their boy, and so nobody has to watch over him. He can watch himself. He's an idle dog, his sisters jokingly claim, as they do their sewing with their aunt, finishing up their work before they can join him in games with the soldiers, constructing for them plays to act and each have a part in.

His sisters are shy, but Branwell will talk to anyone.

His mouth was weak, the line of it, but he'd make up for it moving it.

Their father believes his son is the most gifted. At such an age they all will, now that Maria is gone.

He is a delicate, undersized child who has trouble seeing. He'll need glasses. He has his nervous spells, but he's the favorite of his sisters, the favorite of his father, the favorite of their aunt. He's meant to be their Little King.

Their father would oversee his schooling. The boy's

schooling is that much more important, and his father would not just send him anywhere. He must learn Latin, and he must learn Greek.

They'd have to make something of him.

In Greek, the word Brontë means thunder.

He should display that willpower their father has shown in his own life. This was the way to be honored, respected.

The Latin authors modeled themselves on the Greeks. He's to know that. He's to practice, to model himself, his own writings, on the styles of the classical authors. The boy will learn better at home. Off at school, he'd just have to share his books. He'd have to fit in, and he was not one to fit in.

He'd have to learn to keep up with all the others.

He wouldn't be allowed to develop his expertise.

His father was going to teach him the Classics. They'd work together on lessons in his father's study. With Charlotte, he could share a bit of what he was learning. The light outside was always better than in. They could base the kingdom they ruled over with their soldiers on Greek models, French words they find in other books. Only the two, between them, call it Verdopolis.

It will be like another Athens.

At ten he's reading Virgil and Homer. Branwell and his father work on History. He is their father's hope, their family's hope. Their father gives him the New Testament. But Emily wants to see it.

There's always another Grammar school, in the future, when one he might be ready to be sent off to, so he can learn even more, will reject him. He would not be ready to enter, or to stay very long. He attends Haworth Grammar School for the shortest time, and then he comes back home. His father wants him there. He is better than all those boys, his father tells him, the rough and ready kind. Branwell was going to make more of himself.

They'd read the first six books of the Aeneid, the first four Gospels in Greek, of course they'll read the Iliad, and Horace's Ars Poetica, and Horace's Odes. All these books, their father feels, should have a pleasing effect on his son's morale, will help stabilize his character.

*

If they ever saw he was Irish, they were going to burn him at the stake, in the public square of their village. And through and through, without a doubt, he's Irish. They've created an effigy of him in the village. He knows that likeness is meant to represent him. They would dispose of him by mocking him. That way they could do to him whatever they wanted to do to him. In one hand of the dummy, a potato has been placed. In the other, a herring.

They'd write plays for their soldiers, plays for the Young Men. He and Charlotte would write their Fellows plays. And then their plays of the Islanders. That would give them something to do. They should be allowed to speak, even if they were Irish. He'd write a history of Rebellion. They all know in the village he and his family are really Irish, despite the new last name of Brontë.

The son was the child that looked the most Irish, out of all of them.

The Irish dummy had a shock of bright red atop it.

He was a small boy, sensitive, and delicate; and he wore glasses. His hair was so bright. His face carried all the features of his fatherland, his country.

His hair hung down behind his ears, when he pushed locks of it back, tucked it behind his ears.

He watches from a shop window as villagers burn their Irish effigy. He watches as this likeness of himself, this puppet, their puppet, is carried through the crowd, tossed about by them and trampled.

He was first given the soldiers to play with when Maria, Elizabeth, Charlotte, and Emily left home for school that first time, when only Anne was left home with him, still too young to really play with him. He'd needed something to keep him busy all day.

And when Maria and Elizabeth had died, he'd been given even more sets of soldiers.

Their father could always buy him another.

The ones from before have all been worn out now. Or they've all been broken.

The new ones are more brightly painted. And so they'll get names. They deserve better lives. They're dressed in high black caps, light scarlet jackets, pantaloons, their legs fitted down into their military shoes.

These were the Young Men.

These soldiers had come all the way from Bradford.

The best he'd ever had! A fine body of men indeed. They were his toys, but he'd share them with his sisters, field marshal all of them.

He's like a monster in the morning, in his nightgown, coming up to his sisters' door to show off the new soldiers, to have them grab them all up, to take them with him to go off onto the moors to play. As if they were holding mere mortals in their hands.

They'd give them names and lives based on real people, from battles in the papers. His would be called Bonaparte. But even Bonaparte would have to die. The chronicle they are beginning will be a blending of facts and fiction. They'll come together to bear down on the way the men were to be moved; and they'll have to keep track of it, to keep a record. Branwell will take care of all the battles, since he reads the papers.

Gravey and Waiting-Boy, they are to belong to Emily and Anne. But he and Charlotte have decided they can't really be called that, not real soldiers. They have to be called something like Parry and Ross.

The younger sisters will have to go along with him and Charlotte.

And they could still use Crashey, one of the earlier soldiers, one of the oldest. Their ship is called the Invincible. Charlotte says her soldier is the prettiest of all, tallest, most perfect in everything. They live in glass houses in a glass town. Their childhood would be this imaginary kingdom, as they all must learn to play together. They could write out all their disagreements.

They hadn't yet split the Kingdom up among them. They'd changed the name of their Kingdom at least three times that they now remembered. Emily and Anne hadn't grown up yet, hadn't gone off to man their own world they'd call Gondal, sick of all of Branwell's and Charlotte's wars, leaving them to their Kingdom of Angria then.

Charlotte hadn't yet gone back to school, to become a young lady, eventually a governess.

The climate there was burning, imaginary.

It would be somewhere in the west of Africa, near the delta

26

of the Niger, their Great Glass Town. Look how the glass catches the sun. It bends down off the son's glasses. Their soldiers have shipwrecked on the coast of New Guinea, a place that for more than ten years they will all keep alive, keep going, in one version or another; a City, Kingdom, they'd built.

They would each be Genii, for their favorite soldier, to watch out for him.

They could intervene periodically on the behalf of their own special favorite.

They could bring him back to life.

They were once so close, Charlotte and Branwell, as she'd shared with him the stories of the heroines she'd created to go along with their soldiers. They were beautiful women the men of the Great Glass Town wanted to take away, to have, to hold, and to possess. They were to follow their hearts, each and every one. They couldn't resist the dashing men, according to Charlotte, the venerated soldiers.

And her soldier, the Duke of Wellington, will become the conqueror of Little Branni's soldier Bonaparte. They were his soldiers, but he gave each of his sisters the one they'd picked to be their own.

Their secret Kingdom was being marshaled. It was a harmless game. Scribblemania Branwell would call it. To write, you took some things from real life and you made some up. It all started with the movement of soldiers. They'd be the guarantors, the granters of the existence of their Men, always able to bring casualties back to life. The Genii could influence anything and everyone, the living and the dead. Brannii would be Chief Genius Branwell, Charlotte Tallii. Then came Emmii and Annii.

The empty blue sugar bag on the kitchen floor might be made into the cover for a book. He'd call this his Battle Book. He'd write about the battle of Washington. He'd try to cut all the uninteresting parts out. He might get some facts wrong, but the important thing was that he was writing. He'd work fast. He'd want to have something to show someone, Charlotte. He'd want to be done with it, to show her.

It's only eight pages long. It's only thirty words. But it's his first book, and he's only nine. For more book covers, they could use the wallpaper, too. If they learned to write small enough, then they'd need less pages, less paper. Paper was expensive. When writing this small, it helps to be shortsighted.

He's trying to focus on Culture, not nature. He wants to be a part of Culture, not nature. He wants to enter the world out there in London, the world of writers. He wants to have the adventures of those men they write about. When they are cold and dead and in the grave, this is the only way they'd be remembered.

Or by love.

History of the Rebellion in my Army, that's what he'd write next.

Another early book he'd call The Liar Unmasked.

No, Detected. The Liar Detected.

The passions were the chief thing, in dramatic poetry. And Branwell could still draw pictures in the margins.

Here is the History of what they pretended happened among them, the genesis of the History of the Young Men, their plays.

They were going to give them all a world to live in, to write a place for them, and to care for them by recording their actions. The same things would concern them all. Their civilization begins as a glass town. Then gradually, grandly, how that name has mutated. From this arises their Angria, and eventually Emily's and Anne's own Gondal. Emily and Anne had wanted to write about the moors, not Africa. Charlotte wants to be even more sophisticated, to write about it not just like Africa, but also like France.

Verdopolis, then.

They write books their brother's soldiers could carry, in their little pockets, within which the soldiers could read about their own lives. They had to try hard to make them the right size, to correspond, to make them fit the soldiers. In writing so small their father couldn't see what all his children were trying to say, not with his bad eyes.

The books could be found throughout the house. And the sketches are right there on the walls of their bedrooms, their nursery. All the girls share a room, but he gets his own room down the hall, not too far away from their father.

Their father wanted all their writing in a clear and legible hand. All that was to be written was to be written plainly, so that God could understand it. He'd never know what they were really writing about. Their handwriting gets smaller and smaller, the better his children get at it, the more practiced. And his son Branwell can write with both hands, all at once.

What character out of Aesop's fables does Branwell want to be, if they are each going to get to be one. Charlotte wants to know.

He'll be Boaster.

He can sign whatever he writes with a different name. Call

him Bany-Lightning, but he's many other of the men in Glasstown, too.

It's bedtime, because it's dark outside, but he doesn't want to go to bed. Anything but that.

Then why don't they each have an Island.

His would be the Island of Man.

Next he's to come up with a language the Young Men speak. You held your nose and then you talked. You made the old Young Men's Tongue with all the letters of the Greek alphabet. Branwell is to draw the map of the confederacy that surrounds Glass Town, their capital. They are the guardians of all the soldiers. They have to watch out for them all. His maps are exquisitely detailed. He colors in all the outlines.

*

Every book that came into their hands would be grist for their mill. A little bit was taken from here and there, to make their new time and place.

He had started his own Blackwood's magazine, like the ones their father read, but if he can't do it right, Charlotte is just going to have to take the magazine from him, she says. He could write a concluding address to his readers.

And then she's going to take over.

They could still write some pieces together, too, but he could start a Glasstown newspaper. Why couldn't he just do that.

Or he could concentrate on writing poetry.

Ah, now all seriousness would disappear from the magazine, now that Charlotte's taken over. They'll have smiling faces everywhere.

She says it's not true.

Charlotte is going to write a story about the Little King. He is spoilt and lazy, imperious, unreliable.

He commits violent, unpredictable acts.

And Branwell leaves his shirt open at the neck, to show how he's a poet. Anne only lisps and stutters trying to keep up with him and Charlotte and the fights they have over their little Town.

He is calling his land Sneaky's Land, after Sneaky, who they all know is also Bonaparte.

Young Soult, Soult the Rhymer, is the poet he will begin to write about. You see, Charlotte, in addition to being one of Napoleon's marshals, Young Soult is in actuality the best poet Glass Town has. Branwell's decided it's officially spelled with two words, but when you say it it runs together like one in their Tongue. He knows the true history of Soult because he's seen it all in one of their father's books. His important stories are published in Paris. Chateaubriand will be writing the editorial notes to the celebrated volume.

Charlotte's not sure that's how you spell his name.

He's seen it in one of their father's books.

Charlotte knows he's just writing about himself. He'd started from small beginnings, but his end would be great. Young Soult will be a celebrated poet. He flatters great men one minute and insults them the next.

They won't know what to do with him.

They know Branwell is just dreaming, but sometimes, especially as a child, when one was still one, it was all right to dream.

Emily always believed one must dream.

Charlotte wants to draw Branwell.

He's to sit still while she draws him.

Their brother could be the model for illustrations of the Marshals of Napoleon and for all his relatives.

She could draw him while he's writing. When writing as Captain Bud, he uses many more words than necessary. Because Captain Bud wants to show off his learning. He's the greatest prose writer they have there in all of Glass Town. He knows now it's two words. He's sure.

He asked their father.

You do write it separately.

Young Soult could be rather melodramatic, like Byron, Charlotte says.

Branwell and Charlotte love Byron. And Emily loves him, too.

He drinks too much. And he gambles.

Captain Bud gambles, and it would be the end of his brilliant career.

The Glass Town poet's clothes hung off him, his socks had holes, his shoes were all worn out.

Does Branwell know how to spell the lisp Anne talks with. Does he have any idea. . .

The soldiers are Cracky, Cheeky, Monkey, Goody, Naughty, and Rogue.

Branwell likes Rogue.

They could make a story out of every trip they took, before the characters of Glass Town rebelled.

Glass Town Harbour will become Charlotte's Verdopolis.

They'll all have to start setting their stories there, or come up with something else, if they are all still going to play together, she warns Branwell.

He is still the Chief Genii Brannii. But one day, they will

have to outgrow the Genii, one day soon. He's tired of writing about them.

Then what will they do.

Their soldiers get maimed, burnt, destroyed by other casualties or lost.

When some of the toy soldiers go missing, they send out search parties that must look for them.

The Genii have now appeared for their soldiers, like the Greek gods, each with their mortal to favor.

They watch over them. The soldiers depart sometimes without even a wreck. In all their games, it's a Genius that might eventually destroy them.

Da-da-dum, go their African drums.

Any number of strange things might happen then.

There is the little King, and the little Queens, his sisters.

The King picks violets, surrounded by the young girls he might hire to be his queens, if they are good.

Ceaseless seas of heather.

Heather is not purple.

Don't you know the Genii could make it any color they wanted, Anne. The Genii could bring people back to life again.

Battles and violence, these were all things a healthy boy is to be made of.

For nearly six years, they'd played with nothing but those perennial soldiers. They'd been their horses, when they put them in their pockets.

And for the next thirteen years, they'd write about nothing but them.

Branwell is taking sketches from nature.

The lonely farmhouses. Stone-fenced fields skirt the heather.

There are the ghosts of desire here. They might appear as horses, or dogs, or snakes. They were sudden things that the every day just couldn't account for, that odd feeling that moved over you, as the landscape begins to slip out from under you.

The wooded manors and cloudy skies of England, they believe they'll grow up to live there one day. They hear of them from books he reads to his sisters, as they sewed with their aunt in the parlor, while their father worked away at his sermon.

Branwell never went too far, just to the village.

A walk was a walk through a landscape of moors, glens, and ravines, all glistening with spring or ice, the first hoarfrost.

He'd know the way. He'd know the name of the hills that were to be walked over, know just how high up above the sea they were.

That the air is salted by that.

It is his job to escort his sisters, when they want to go out. The little and lone green lane leads from the parsonage out to and over the moors, finally giving way to the vaster wilderness.

He'd place stepping stones down for them, so they could all ford the stream. He'd help each of them across. Here, Charlotte, give him your hand.

What a gentleman!

Branwell is blushing, bowing, Anne and Emily laughing.

Emily wants to try crossing by herself, no stones.

They'll go to their waterfall.

The waterfall is where man's mind can run away with itself.

They still believe they see intelligence sparkling in their brother's eyes, behind his glasses.

His hair's not red, it's auburn. When he gets older, he'll tramp these fields, with a gun in his hand. Once he gets tall enough, he believes he might be able to embark on a real military career. If only he had a horse to ride, one day. He'll have to be disciplined.

They visit the library at Ponden Hall. They walk there. It's on the Heatons' land, a great paneled room on the second floor of a great house. It is here he'd become familiar with Chateaubriand and his book of traveling in Greece, Palestine, Egypt, the Holy Lands, and Barbary.

The Heaton boys, the children of this family, are their playmates sometimes.

It's here that they could read Shakespeare.

There were rules for making verses, ways to conjure sublime thoughts. There were allusions. There was a dictionary of words that rhymed, when rhyme was to take the place of reason.

It's here they'd become more precocious, intoxicated by all the books.

It's carpeted in red, a palace. Crimson, Branwell calls it. The tables and chairs are all covered in this rich way to match, the pure white ceiling bordered with gold. They stretch out on the lushness of the carpet, when the chairs get too much for them. When they go to dream a scene up onto the ceiling, what will they see.

The glass and silver chandelier is one intricate flower, upturning itself over them, lighting them up, the steady glow of the soft taper stamen.

It's like they're in Heaven.

It's there for them anytime they want.

In reality, outside of the books, Ponden Hall is more a farmhouse than a mansion, made of its green-gray slabs of stone.

Emily will remember it always, though, Heaton, Hareton, Heathcliff. She makes rhyming words run their way through the carpet.

There are ghosts outside in the garden.

Branwell says he hears them crying, even now. You just had to listen closely.

And they'll all come back, the ghosts of this place, just as soon as the Heaton boys have died, like their sisters, as soon as the day comes when grass begins to grow up unchecked between the flags, so tall. As soon as everyone else has gone.

He's telling Emily stories again. He's slept one night in a haunted house with a man he met in the village, to see if the bed did really move all by itself in the middle of the night. Or if the candle went from here to there.

They'd bend over their books in the library, and then look up amazed to see how much time had passed over, just like that. You could tell by the clock over the Heaton chimney.

It would be dark outside, now.

But Branwell is there with them, to walk them home.

As long as they are all holding hands, the sky can still appear benign, no matter how dark, moths like little ghosts, just barely discernible under a moon pulled into itself.

Our moor is here, under a rolling expanse of gray sky.

There's the sound of the wind in the grass, and their shoes.

They're walking back over where one day they'll rest for good.

*

Their brother would be trained to be an artist. They must coax his hidden talent out into full bloom. He must be driven enough, in imagination, talented enough to support them all.

If their father dies, what would they do.

Branwell hasn't yet made a fortune at the age of twelve, even though he's started his own Blackwood's magazine for them. All he has to do is copy. He can always write about war and power and taking over, taking control, even if he can't really do it. The Little King in his story wields a large black club. Glory is to be written about, and fame. Far afield must reach the name. At fourteen, he knows that.

An end must approach now to all old institutions, authorities and opinions. This spells a revolution for the son. A son of England! No matter he's Irish. Hadn't the poet Shelley championed their people. He'd make them listen. Their father tells him they have God on their side. They'd be protected, from the frightening prospect of gore, rumor, glory. Tolerance, virtue, and wisdom must be practiced.

A rebel, with a homeland.

He'll be like Shelley. Emily likes Shelley, too.

The boy is to be indulged.

He finds the house boring while his sisters are all about their cleaning up. The house where they live is too small for him. He doesn't want to be around while his sisters do the chores their aunt assigns. Emily and Anne sit down to the table together, in the parsonage, to help peel potatoes.

He needs some friends of his own sex. There were the village boys, but their father doesn't want his son fooling around with them. He doesn't want his son drinking. He has had his own problems with such.

Inside the bar, his son would become very popular with the boys, as he talked a way none of them could, entertained them. He talked a purple streak.

He's just watering himself in the bar, whetting his appetite. He's still going to be somebody someday.

At ten, he was writing before his sisters.

He was the boy, so he's learned everything first.

In him, his sister Charlotte thinks she sees her mental equal.

Home instruction given by their father has prepared him for nothing, except for perhaps one day tutoring boys as he himself had been tutored, or going into the Church. The larger world, the wider world, it so tempts and scares him, and their father still wants to keep him close.

Branwell has good stories to tell at the bar.

His father doesn't want him playing with the village kids ever, not unless they are boys who go to Sunday School. They'll rough him too much, coarsen him, corrupt the training their father instilled in him.

He'd learn to trade in an inferior, debased currency.

They don't wear the white cravats his father wears, none of those men in the bar.

The men in the bar liked Branwell.

He's so pleasingly handsome to watch. Look at the way he talks.

He looks a little taller, because the last time he'd gone with his father to the barber, he'd had his red hair crested up a bit.

They could all draw pictures of their soldiers inside the front cover of his Latin New Testament, their soldiers standing under the trees with their swords. If men laid on their stomachs, then they'd be snuck up on and eaten by the animals. There were lots of blank pages at the back of the Classical Geography, from which his father was now trying to teach him, for even more pictures. Their father would never look at the back. SATURN, SATAN, SATURN, Branwell writes in dark capitals.

And they could write in from the margins, too, fill them all up.

They were to study, to read, to sketch, copy anything, any pictures from books, to be artists, the engravings on the wall, to keep themselves busy.

His companion Charlotte was soon to be sent off to school, again, and he'd begun to draw up into himself, as Emily and Anne would continue their own game of writing together. It's not Angria with them, but Gondal.

He's had Charlotte to write with, Charlotte who wouldn't be there now, Charlotte who was going off to school just as Maria had. He was fifteen.

*

Death was everywhere, he believed, if you only went looking for it.

Branwell sketches his profile in the graveyard.

While Charlotte was away at school, he'd begin writing, begin developing, Alexander Rogue. Alexander Rogue has red hair, too. He's over six feet tall. Rogue was about to start a civil war. Glass Town would be full of war for a while.

He'd now be able to give a bit more free reign to his hand.

But maybe Alexander Percy was a better name.

Colonel the Honourable Alexander Augustus Percy is an ex-pirate. A bit unbalanced and obsessed, he'll be the Earl of Northangerland, by Branwell's command. Civil wars erupt in his name.

They would eventually have to sentence a man like him to the firing squad. But he himself would give the order to shoot: the Earl of Northangerland decrees, shoot him.

And there's hanging for his cohorts, after the third degree.

He'd never be able to gather together political, domestic, and amorous intrigue, not as finely as Charlotte anyway.

Branwell imagined an immortal man, standing before them all, tall and solemn, no hat on his head, his features paled, eyes sunken in his intensity. He'd dress him in a black frock coat, trousers, a red ribbon wrapped tightly around his neck that matched the shade of scarlet his lips took on, as he rubbed them against the back of his hand. His eyes stared darkly out at all before him, his hair uncut and unkempt. It floated wildly about him, in the moor winds. His cheeks had hollowed out in desire, in his eyes the light of madness.

And Branwell would carry a kitchen knife, up his coat sleeve, just in case he came across anything he shouldn't out on the moors, man or beast.

When he met a man, he'd hold his hand tightly in the shake while at the ready with the weapon concealed.

Charlotte wants to read more, more about this rogue. He'd write more for her.

Alexander Rogue, believed dead, was really living like a prince, in a fine house in George's Street. In London, Branwell believes.

And he was a drinker.

Even in those classics, begrudgingly approved by their father, alcohol was a backdrop, a source of inspiration. Branwell's decided to start wearing his red hair long like a poet, an artist, a genius.

He's begun entertaining them down around and in the Black Bull, while Charlotte's away, while their father keeps himself shut up in his study, while Emily and Anne play together, writing. There was life, vibrant to a boy, at the Black Bull. He's to be found there when not over lessons with his father. That little bit of talent he might have, they don't want him to squander it.

He lives in a fantasy world he doesn't want to advance too far from, where he'll always have an audience. He could help those men with their bottles.

Listen to him. Listen to what he's just written.

But publishing editors wouldn't be so interested in him. They wouldn't be so interested in Charlotte either, not her romances. Poor girl, they'd call her among themselves. She and Branwell had begun sending all their fantastic stories out, soliciting opinions. His sister Charlotte would be persistent. She wouldn't give up. She'd keep writing. That's the mark of a real writer. And one day Charlotte would eventually get the response she's been waiting for. One day everyone in the family would gather around her, as she's gotten a letter from a famous man!

She knows the work she's sent him is early work, but she had more plans. That story there was just the start of something much bigger.

41

At nineteen, a poet didn't need to be published. Branwell goes to the bars like the Black Bull and the White Lion.

He holds forth there. Just listen to that Irish lilt he lifts his voice up in! Ringing through the bar, as it had once rung through their house, Branwell reading out loud and loud to Charlotte as she worked around the parsonage.

They believe the boy has been blessed with a gift.

They laugh in approval, and he believed he knew exactly where he stood.

*

Leaving the three of them back behind, at fifteen Charlotte had gone off to school, venturing out into the world for a second time.

He must know that he's still everything to her.

Even though she's gone off to school, they could still write Angria together. Whenever they were unhappy, their Angria was a place they could always return to. She was not going to leave him alone in a flaming sunset. She writes these romantic words. To him she sends letters, poems, sketches. All things for Angria.

Though off at school, she still thought of all of them there home at Haworth, Emily and Anne, deep in their twin Gondal.

Branwell must write to her about what's been happening in Angria.

He could share her last letter with everyone.

They'd keep in touch, through this writing. He'd write The History of the Young English Men. He'd fill six notebooks with his Letters from an Englishman. She writes to ask him, is he still reading Blackwood's. Has he been able to get his hands on anything else in the little moorland village where their father had set up house for them.

And their father, how was his health. Was the weather still wearing at it, taking its toll. Their aunt, was she any happier, now that pleasant Spring seemed imminent. He'd write her letters, wouldn't he, and tell her of any changes he's making to their Angria.

She wants him to know how his letters soothed her, and how much they delighted her, like music she carried around in her head with her during the days.

He'd walked twenty miles just to see Charlotte at Roe Head and twenty miles back.

He was her very dear brother, with his delicately humped nose and soft sideburns. He was still a facet of her very soul.

He'd surprise her.

They were to be together.

There's a tree there, that lightning has split, but see how it still grows. It still grows green. They were in ecstasies with the woods, walking holding hands. How she enjoyed the charms of his society!

She knows her brother is to be so many things.

And she'll be anxious to know he got home safe, walking back all that way. She'd have to write to him to find out. He's bound to be very tired, walking all that way. But he hadn't complained at all.

He's used to running across the moors, so his legs are strong. His legs are used to it, he says. She knows he's tired, even though he wouldn't tell her he was.

Excitement holds a man up.

Only after he'd left, then did she remember all the things she had wanted to ask him.

She remained his affectionate sister.

He was the one who was going to accomplish all the things that the rest of them would not be able to do.

When Charlotte comes home, she'll try to teach her sisters. And if Charlotte teaches where she's once studied then Emily can come for free as a student.

She writes home to her brother.

With no homework left, up there alone in the dormitory, she's taken up their chronicle of Angria again. The men of their stories are to be great men, men of accomplishment all. You see, dear brother, you can't desert her. You could not believe what she's had to go through, how she knows they just want to make her like them, a part of a proper set, an object.

They were all so self-righteous. If only you could see them.

She doesn't want to ever disappoint him. It was he who had pointed out the chestnut tree she'd one day be able to use, in writing, as the symbol of a love despite all, opening to everything. He's the one who knows who she was, deep down inside herself. All those letters they'd written back and forth, about all their characters, about the newspapers and the books their characters read, they'd kept each other sharp, on their feet, for the detail. In inspiration she'd begun pacing.

If he could only hear what she's just written. If only she could have seen him then, read to him her latest. Her heart goes hot in this place. Branwell was a darling. She hadn't wanted to leave him. It was the thought of him, his understanding, that had always given her strength.

*

He writes to Charlotte at Roe Head, as she's now teaching, how their Zamorna has destroyed his palace, and he has burned Adrianopolis.

Reader, these were wonderful times, times of change. Change was coming, bloody change. A long civil war, from a distance.

He's placed her favorite character in the worst military crisis of his career.

He's written The Rising of the Angrians, nineteen to Charlotte's twenty, to try and finish off their saga once and for all. It needs the perfect ending. The men of Glass Town are changing. They are outcasts, pirates, soldiers, conquerors, murderers, all the things men are driven by history to be remembered as.

They love money and they need money.

He writes the stories, and then he illustrates them.

Or he draws the picture first and then writes the story, enclosing himself in a cycle. Just look at all he's accomplished in this last year. Charlotte was going to have to try to keep up with him.

Sometimes out at night, out at the Black Bull, up in the upper room, or down at the old White Lion, Branwell will try his hand at boxing. The struggle in the ring gets out the aggression. If Charlotte could see him here, staring at the broadness of the chests of other men, she might make fun of him. But she knows if he hurts his right hand boxing, he can always just write with the left, until it gets better.

The men there see his brilliance, potential, his personal charms, and they'll testify to it. Boxing with other men only

45

strengthens your body. Byron himself had been deeply fascinated with the sport.

All the other members of the Boxing Club work. Branwell doesn't have to yet, as his father is still instructing him.

She had left him. His partner Charlotte. She had her school, teaching. There's that new empty place in the house now with her not there.

He's to become more independent because of this, more a man.

One day he wouldn't need her at all. One day he would need not to, even if one day she did come back home.

*

There are the black woods. He sketches them. He makes more sketches. He has begun to assess the mediocrity of himself in these surroundings. It might be different if he could transform it more.

He was born in a miserable little village. He dreams of seeing the world, of the world opening up her arms to him. He refuses to be insignificant.

How is he to try to continue to enter further into life, outside their bars. It's once he sees himself becoming a man, needing to become more of one, and what that could mean, that he might begin to feel his own lack.

A boy like him needed heroes to worship, someone to keep aspiring to be. There's an ideal hero that could be arrived at in the poem. Though not intended to be an exact portrait, there are obviously some similarities. In some ways, he believes he and his heroes resemble each other.

Besides his Alexander Percy, Earl of Northangerland, he's written his Captain John Flower, the Right Honorable John Baron Flower. A Viscount, an M.P.—Branwell designates the men he plays to be such things. All it takes is a stroke from his pen. Henry Hastings, the ladies mocked him. But there's still Warner Howard Warner, who's not just a milk and water man. He turned violently red, if you ever tried to scold him.

Flattery, that's what a soldier needed.

The men in such stories swept over lands and oceans.

His poems would be epics. He'd emphasize action, as the only boy of six children. He has to do something. His paintings, when he starts to paint, will be huge canvases. They'd have to be, crumbling under the scrutiny of a corrective perspective. They will not cohere exactly, or hold up much outside of novelty.

Right now he's just sketching.

And then the men he writes, they could always just be killed, if not rescued, from situations his pen put them in.

Destruction was a way of life.

He wakes to find himself tied to a table, a character he's writing, the top and floor covered in blood that has dried deep red. He's been dissected alive, he suddenly understands, and faints away.

Only one way for men to act.

Now he wants to be a man named Richton. It's not too late to try to change his character.

Branwell has decided he wants to be a painter, not a writer. For his sister Anne, he'll sketch a castle and a tower, something she could still write about even in Gondal. A round tower, a ruined tower. There were such things there, surely. A scene in a neighboring farmyard suggests another sketch. He'll sketch the cat sleeping curled up in the field, careful not to wake her. He sketches a warrior all clad in mail, calls this drawing Terror.

See, he likes Anne, too.

He titles a watercolor he's done The Hermit.

He's begun one of a man in a turban, reading.

And he could be a musician, too. He's bought a book of flute music.

*

Everyone wants Branwell to be an artist, when he begins to practice with paints. And he won't be just a sign-painter. They all believe he should go to the Royal Academy. Charlotte can work hard at a job of governess to help support him. Sacrifices will be made for him. There must be. He'd need to live in London.

At the back of their kitchen is the old peat storeroom, a pantry of sorts, and it's just big enough to be converted into a studio for him to work in, to practice painting in. They all believe now this is what Branwell will make of himself. Even his aunt.

And with a little to drink, he could stay in there for a long time.

But they aren't to know he's drinking in there.

He can hear his father in the other room committing another sermon to memory. They are pinning their hopes on Branwell, all of them.

He's to paint his three sisters in preparation for his life of artistic promise, after the country scenes he's learned to draw at first by mimicking from others' engravings in books.

Charlotte will compare him favorably to other famous painters. Though he still draws better than he paints.

Their father has hired a painting Master to come and teach his son. A Mr. Robinson will teach him. Mr. William Robinson must be paid for each visit, but he's a professional who's painted the Duke of York, the Princess Sophia, and even the very real Duke of Wellington.

Branwell is not as good as his other students, but he might be taught, Mr. William Robinson believes. Branwell is to listen to him and do everything he says.

But Branwell would not. Branwell would not just let himself blossom. You had to trust your teachers. That's the only way. Surely Mr. William Robinson knows more than him. Can there be any doubt. Look at all he's already painted, done. He has a job. He teaches young boys like Branwell, shows them what they might make of their talent. He was here to try and help Branwell make it in the world. It was up to him, through him, Branwell must listen to him, enough, to see how he'd fit one day into the landscape of painters, or perhaps, in Branwell's case, draughtsmen.

Here Mr. William Robinson put his hand on the shoulder of his young charge.

Mr. William Robinson of Leeds, his eyes could pierce right through you.

That's how you'll ask them all to pose when they come to sit for you.

You'll wear a dark coat like Mr. William Robinson.

Go outside and sit like this.

Now look over there.

Have them look away, and then while they hold their gaze in the way you've directed it up, yes, see, you can move their shoulders back like this, tip their chin just so, you can, no, move your, your chest, your chest just needs to be touched, relaxed, pushed back just a bit.

There. That's all. Just like that. It all happens that quick.

And then does Branwell see what he's pointing to up in the sky, up where Robinson wants him holding his gaze. Does Branwell feel something, something different, anything in his stomach. Like a bird in his stomach, turning in circles, head tucked up under its wing, touching his insides.

He can't see what's before him that way, while trying to fly, what one must go through.

In reality they'd get nowhere like that.

He would paint his sisters, all three of them, around this time.

For a time he struggled with this. Even at eighteen, he's not a good painter yet. He paints himself with a gun.

Now he wasn't to paint his sisters too ugly.

What would be the best way to arrange them all in a portrait. He paints them all with the eyes of rabbits, glazed over in a fear. He paints that there. He puts them almost in tears. He had begun to paint himself in there along with them, all arranged around him, and now he has just given up.

He's not going to be able to live up to their image of him.

They could all be seated around a table, or standing up.

He gives Charlotte the most firmly set mouth. He paints Emily with more sensuousness. He had himself initially standing up behind them, but he looked like the one thing that didn't belong. One could see how if he'd just remove himself, the painting might appear more balanced. He didn't fit with his sisters, where Emily has been placed in shadows, Anne resting her head on her shoulder, Charlotte lit with something like the sun.

A breeze in the portrait will touch only Emily.

The next time he paints her, he'll give Emily an even nicer dress.

One day Charlotte will have this painting to keep.

He's been removed, for the sake of making a better picture, and the composition overall is indeed better without him. That pillar there in the center instead will take his place. A cross divides the canvas into the scope of fields, how it must have been folded in on itself once to protect it when there was no frame.

Over time, the self he's tried to cover over in the painting of his sisters by the placement of the centered pillar, will come to light; as the oil paint slowly gains more transparency, the older and older it gets, his figure, a fourth, emerges between them, ever more visible beneath the pillar of separation painted down the middle, becoming him.

*

In the Winter he could take more lessons from Mr. William Robinson, nearly completing the picture he's to be judged on, if he's ever to go to the Royal Academy. They will have to find the money somewhere. His aunt could help. Perhaps she could. She's like a mother to him.

He wants to finish the picture of Maria he's started trying to call up, but she still looks too much like an indistinct composite, a doll.

Mr. William Robinson will have to instruct him further in Anatomy, when his father is not giving him more Horace poems to work on translating, before Branwell goes off to London, to begin his career.

Can Mr. William Robinson tell Mr. Brontë if he should really be kept on.

The boy's forms were crudely delineated. His colorations were uninspired. He was a fine draughtsman, but as for what truly animates life, he appears to not have grasped properly yet how to mix one's pigments. There are ways one is to use them correctly. One day his colors won't seem to be real flesh.

He's never done exactly what Mr. William Robinson has told him to do. And there are some things, even he, Mr. William Robinson, doesn't know. Over time, the appearance of blood in even Mr. Robinson's pictures was just going to fade. He didn't know how to teach him. It's light and shade that makes a real portrait.

London was far away, farther away than the villages close by Branwell had been to occasionally with his father. In Liverpool, that's where one could buy Byron's book, Childe Harold's Pilgrimage. He'd be able to do things there one could do only in cities. London had haunted all of their minds for such a long time. Branwell had studied maps to memorize it, so it would be as if he'd always lived there, once he got there. He'd know all the streets by heart.

Instinctively, one fears ending pleasure by approaching the reality.

This was the place he'd been reading all about. The crowds would press in on him. But he believes by studying maps he knows a short cut, just up that narrow lane there, one or two back streets.

He might be able to right himself there in London. They're fearing for his future, already, his sisters. What should Branwell do. If he went to London in September, the Royal Academy would be closed.

It's Charlotte who had drawn first, who first had the idea

to trace the pictures from all their books. Together with Charlotte, they'd copied engravings from all the books, another skill they believed might help in preparing them for life. She and Branwell would be most talented at this copying, and when they'd run out of pictures in books, they'd copy engravings from the Parsonage walls. There's one of the end of the world. Another of the Devil's face. If they ever wanted to teach, they'd all need skills, if they were ever going to be able to earn their keep in this world. They have to copy carefully, every line, every detail.

Eventually they would be able to do it even without a model. Every leaf of the book must be traced. The world might be studied and felt through this perspective.

They were creating their own world, a world below the outside world, an infernal one, because it is not God's, a kingdom their father approves.

His children must learn to save themselves from the world outside their books.

Their aunt had a little savings she could give their brother for his trip to London. He'll leave with just enough money to support himself for a month or two, until he gets settled.

Though he never really attempts to enter school there, Branwell, they believe, does indeed go off to London.

It will take two days just to get there.

He'll be sent off in a coach.

He shakes in the coach, as if setting off on the ocean, to the Continent, a new life. It pulls him away from the land he's known, his family, that sunlight cresting in the sky.

Mr. William Robinson had encouraged him, hadn't he. Mr. William Robinson had touched him and told him he was a strong boy. He had to make his way, Charlotte had said repeatedly. He is making his way out into the world now. He'll have to be good enough to get into the school in London, if he wants to stay there.

It's the landscape around him that begins to rage, then, and the further he gets from home, the more foreign the soil becomes. Games of his past must be left back there now. Emily and Anne are at home writing their Gondals. He's alone in the carriage. His father has given him a piece of advice. As he goes deeper into an Autumn landscape less recognizable, Branwell must think of the talk his father had given him of the nuts that must be gotten at through hard work, a cracked shell. Branwell must see that, the outside was what you had to get through.

The ground begins to slide away from under him, like the day he and Emily and Anne had just escaped, while out for a walk, all his other sisters off at school, all of them still living.

He can't remember if their mother was still, too.

Their father had thought he might have lost them, all of them in that natural disaster, pressure building up underground, the bog erupting. Their father's sermon that Sunday had been on that. The redness in the sky, it had warned their father of the harm that might come to his children out there all alone. The deadly tree of knowledge was waiting for his only son.

The trees swept over the carriage, drowning him down in the pull of light green through them.

An entire stone bridge was nearly swept away that day. In the gathering, turbulent darkness, bridges were damaged. His heart had begun to thunder in his chest.

He'd not yet made it to London.

Listening to his father's warnings, he'd trembled all day that day.

The earth rolled out under the carriage like the tide taking him out. Rooks, seagulls dipped by the windows, birds that don't know their names. A heron, a bee, beat in his pulse.

And then cows in the fields where they are supposed to be.

He'd practiced a draft of his letter to the secretary of the Royal Academy on the back of a poem he was working on. Where was he to present his drawings. When. And at what time.

What was this feeling in his stomach, like a snake now coiled there inside, its skin cool as if wet.

London, this was the city he was supposed to love.

He was finally going there, that great, big place.

He'd been studying maps in his room, had learned all the routes. He'd been learning them ever since he and Charlotte began the imaginary Kingdom. Now that place he could make spring up for him back home seems more real than London.

One of the things he'd done when at the Black Bull had been to give men passing through directions on how to get about London most quickly. That was one of the things he could talk to them about.

It will all come as an affront, the sudden, new environment, the truth of London.

All he really knew was at his home with his sisters.

Does he have his letters of recommendation in his pocket, from Mr. William Robinson. Branwell has letters of introduction to many people, people who can help him, people he only had to call on, any number of people.

In the presence of patently successful people, he could find himself totally at a loss.

They might not take him.

Did he still have the rough map his father has drawn up for him, to help guide him where he'll be lodging, once he gets there. He'll be staying where his father has once or twice. But that first night there in the room, he won't sleep or even undress.

He was going to make his way down the Embankment, to gaze at the traffic down on the river, all of it, the sun shining on him there, lighting up his clothes. He would have one drink in the big city. He feels less substantial on these streets in all his apparent poverty. Look how he's dressed. How was he supposed to present himself to people of quality in such a state.

He carries along with him in the streets of London a mortified pride.

Look at the carriage he had come in, like the dog cart they'd once had to drive in, he and his sisters, when going to visit friends of Charlotte, all so much better off than they. The Brontës were obviously from the country.

They were all looking at him. But they won't waste too much time on him.

They all have their own business in London.

He's in London! He recognizes names of places. The torrent of the city will sweep him away from all he's known, and all the motion begins to depress.

He's going to have a drink, but not rum. He hates rum.

What will it be, then. Whisky, followed by gin. There are still other sights to see.

56

There's a tavern called the Castle in High Holborn, run by a boxer everyone knows by name, Tom Spring. Once a famous boxer, he's now bar owner. He made his way into all the books and magazines on boxing and London Branwell had read. The Castle was a place where Branwell himself might become more of a character.

The bar is full of boxers. He's read about such places in Bell's Life in London. They're all just waiting for the next fight, drinking rum, whisky, gin. They have the arms of blacksmiths. Branwell wouldn't even be able to fit his hand around them. He could try.

Painters also came to Tom Spring's, to look over the currently retired or available pugilists as possible models. Boxers are a most excellent subject. Just ask any Academy teacher worth his salt.

There was no street entrance to the Castle. You have to come inside through the coach entrance door. The filth and dazzle of London fully seethes over the sorrows. He knows all the streets. A few nights there might last one man a lifetime. For some, one night will have to be enough. Any robust, kindly company will be a comfort to him.

If they'd like to hear, if there is any question, he knows the dates of a lot of battles. All of his money could be spent in this bar, on, with, around boxers. Remember that. Trivia that men bat back and forth. One never got true happiness without working for it.

In London he meets a man named Woolven. He'd have to return home in about a week, but he and Woolven could remain friends.

Where he fits in London is in the boxer's bar, the Castle, not some gallery, the Royal Academy, studying pictures. He'll tell his family he's been robbed, to explain how his money has all gone missing for nothing.

And the news will spread over Haworth. It would spread like wildfire, down around the Black Bull. They'd held him against a wall, those sharpers. That's what they called them there in London. They'd reached for his money, put their hands down in his pockets.

Branwell has not been able to take a hold of his own destiny, yet, but give the boy time.

There was the National Gallery, where he'd never live to see his pictures. One couldn't have come to London without seeing it. He was just going to run up the stairs, up into the museum, quickly, to get it all over with.

The lowest step of the museum was kissed, before he'd left.

And he would have had to visit Westminster Abbey.

It was a writer he was meant to be. He could see that now.

Later, Branwell would be able to sketch the Abbey from memory, once he got back home.

He'd need a new character when he returned, a new one to write about and to give adventures like his own in London. He'd write Charles Wentworth lying in London on the sofa in his hotel room, unable to move further after a quick, initial sightseeing, Mr. Charles Wentworth, who had just visited Verdopolis, the huge, consuming space he is too afraid to get lost in.

The roof of reality was vast. Would his sisters ever be able to really understand the sublime dome. There were temptations one didn't dare speak of or succumb to, unassisted.

His family will never be able to trust him again. Not off in London again, where he'd been skinned of every last penny.

He returned home after a few days.

His sister Charlotte was still off at Roe Head, governessing, and he could feel their father's blue eyes boring into him. It seemed after all that he was not to be a pupil at the Royal Academy.

*

Instead he'd go each week over to Mr. William Robinson's studio in Leeds. It's cheaper than Mr. William Robinson coming to him at Haworth. In Leeds, they'd be working from a live model. Branwell could stay in the inn for the night, up for his lessons, one night a week away from home.

Would his aunt help pay for that.

He's going to become a portrait painter, so one day they don't have to worry about what they're going to do when they no longer have a father, or the mercy of the church. Emily, she wants to stay at home, where she has her dog. But she can come visit him in Bradford, for his birthday. In Bradford, they have hotels with nice lounges, and you could drink there.

In Bradford he first tried opium. You could get it over the counter, from a chemist. He should try it. There had been books about it, poems about it. He had a friend in Bradford. They could do it together one night, with each other. It cost less than alcohol. It lasted longer.

It would help him not die so young, as his sisters Maria and Elizabeth had. Those who swore by it said such.

And the more opium Branwell took, the longer he could try to paint, once back home, in the little room where they'd once stored the peat.

Branwell might one day still look for somewhere else to live, a little studio in Bradford.

John Brown, the sexton, would come to be painted.

Though Charlotte and Anne were off at school, they were all still together, all in spirit, in that little house. Charlotte was teaching. Anne was a student, and Emily wanted to stay home.

John was to dress in his Sunday best for Branwell.

Nobody would be able to smell the opium on his breath. In liquid form, they taught him in Bradford, they call it laudanum. Now things were more vivid, the presence of objects near more exaggerated, the outlines of people, places, things more indistinct, as if lost a bit in golden mist, as he tried to pin the sun of a summer shining down on the canvas, alone in his room, a world of wild roses opening up under the yellow.

And there's the tic he has in his face. The opium is good for that, too, they tell him.

To the streets of Bradford, that's where artists go. It's the city nearest Haworth, nearest home. That's where you'd have to go if you wanted to be a painter. That's where there are boys in the street who gather all around him, and he jokes with the little ruffians, giving them pennies, when pennies still mean something.

All their father's friends could come get their portrait painted by Branwell in Bradford, all the men from the Church.

Then he could walk home on the weekends, eight miles, to visit his family.

If they could still see him on the weekends, they could feel he was adjusting fine to separation.

A year almost elapsed while he tried to paint portraits in Bradford, living with a Mr. and Mrs. Kirkby, before returning home. The return would be a blow, but once there he believed there might be some comfort. The opium makes his thoughts larger, longer, softer, more caressing, surrendering vision, when in doubt.

Back home, alone, he and his father study some more, to try to have him better prepared next time he goes out into the world. The boy just needs to decide what he really wants to do. If he just wanted to be a tutor, they might find him a post.

There were lots of rich people to paint in Bradford, or so he'd believed. The room he'd rented in Bradford had been both his studio and his bedroom. It was on Fountain Street. His lodgings had been genteel and comfortable, well suited for the single gentleman, or a lady and a gentleman, if they might share a bed. Just at the foot of his studio stairs was the George Hotel bar where the artists, and businessmen, gathered. There were landscape painters, engravers, sculptors, portrait painters like Branwell, even future historians.

There was a sculptor who had done a Satan, who had dark eyes, a mocking expression, a powerful, heavily built frame.

Lucifer, he's also the morning star.

They'd become friends.

He wanted someone to talk to, and society at the George was bold, daring, masculine. He had become quite a character around those parts.

Branwell was one of the poets. He entertained them in the pub, just as he had back home at the Black Bull, in amongst crowds of men. He knew how to hold their attention, speaking of his friend's sculpture, Venus, the star

Lucifer, words brought to life in stone. He was good and practiced in this light.

Charlotte had come to visit him there, in Bradford. She'd see. Lying around the room were all the canvases he'd started. One day he'd finish one. The women he painted all just looked like earlier pictures he'd painted of them, his sisters. But the men he's started, he seems troubled to make them all appear more distinct.

Charlotte believes he was acting just a little bit curious, but his landlady's niece seems to like him.

They notice he likes to paint well-to-do men.

He'd practiced already at home on one who'd gone on to become a mill owner. He used to be his friend. There was a well-known Haworth tenor, the brandy merchant, and more mill owners. But commissions in Bradford had not come in like he'd hoped. Nowadays everybody was beginning to go in for their daguerreotypes.

The George Hotel bar was full of men like Branwell. In Bradford, portrait painters swarmed everywhere, and he was just going to have to do varnish work for other painters who had been more fortunate, if he couldn't get portrait commissions.

*

One day their father would die. Already he eats alone in the other room, in his study, says he has to. He says he needs the perfect quiet for his digestion, shuts himself up in there, year after year consigned to his room no one's to go in except for lessons. Branwell will be in there with him then.

If Branwell couldn't support them, it would be a job left

for Charlotte. They wouldn't want to deny Branwell his fondest wishes. Branwell was going to take his dinner tonight at the Black Bull. Charlotte was going to teach, to put up the money for Branwell to have more painting lessons, for art school in London; because he's shown promise. Then, she could work towards the completion of her younger sisters' educations.

He could just try to forget about London, those dreams, going back to there after Bradford, after honing his talents as a painter. He could have made a study tour of the Continent, but he'd need the full backing of his father. They try to hide their disappointment with him, but he can tell.

There were many things he could always be at home. He could join the Freemasons, at their Haworth Lodge. He's too young by their normal standards, but they must certainly respect his father.

What does the boy do.

He was going to become a portrait painter.

One couldn't spit at that.

The Lodge of the Three Graces, the Freemasons. They would meet at the Black Bull Tavern for their annual dinner on St. John's Day. Branwell could be their Secretary, Organist, and their Junior Warden. He could lead their toasts. He could work his way up to the degree of Fellowcraft, and then shortly after that, if he played his cards right, he could become a Master Mason.

His father will encourage him. His father won't give up on him.

There with the Masons he will have his much-needed male companionship. The Masons were very much a secret society, so he's not allowed to talk to anyone about what happens there, he must promise, even to his sisters. Not even to his father. His father is not a mason, though respected. He's not like the sexton. Their next door neighbor, the sexton John Brown, is this chapter's Master.

It is a leap year, the year Branwell enters their ranks. A man guards the door, a Brother, during secret meetings. There's an initiation involved. Was he prepared to go through with it. Does he truly want it. Does he really know, grasp, everything for which the Freemasons stand.

Was Branwell willing to try to find out.

He must empty his pockets of anything he might have in them, and he must open his shirt so that his left breast may be exposed. There, before them, he must roll up his shirt so they can see his right arm. And they want to see next his right knee. Loosen his right shoe.

He won't know where they are taking him, who they are taking him to.

He doesn't know all about their ranks yet. They are just preparing him.

He's not supposed to tell anyone how they blindfold him, about the rope that is slipped down around his neck. They pull the cord that feels as tight as a noose.

Will they lead him by this fashioned leash, wherever they are taking him.

He feels something cold suddenly against his breast, sharp, unyielding, and substantial, like metal; this point pricks him when he moves against it. He backs up. He has to be careful. Branwell could hurt himself if he's not.

There's a little laughter, and solemnity he can't see but can make out in the air, the way the room seems to shift about him, outside the binding around his eyes. He had come here of his own free will, to be accepted into their ranks. Hadn't he. Soon he would be able to partake of the privileges of Masons, all the mysteries.

They must ask now for God's blessing, as he kneeled down before someone, the Master. But he couldn't know yet who the Master was. He's pulled back to his feet, led around, blindfolded, inside what must be a very large room. They want all the members to get a good look at him, in his state of ignorance, blinded, before he is truly one of them. Only if he is unworthy of them would he ever tell what has happened there among them.

They ask him what he wishes for, and then he gives them the right answer. Branwell answers light.

After he swears to all the oaths, the God-given rights of their sect, they will remove the bandage from around his eyes, and Branwell will see.

You would never expect that these were the men who would be here, from the places they normally occupied in Haworth. Their neighbor John Brown himself is the worshipful Master.

Branwell is now an Entered Apprentice. John Brown calls him by this name. Here is how he was to take, hold, shake their hands. Each and every one of them. There's a grip specific to them.

He can get dressed now.

It is a sword they've held to his breast.

He'll be so much closer to John after this.

How does he feel.

Drinks were passed around. There are five degrees of fellowship, these acceptable ways to show joy and to exalt in each other's presence. Once he's learned them all, he'll advance in his rank.

John Brown strokes him across the forehead, Brontë's little boy.

There is another Mason ceremony where Branwell is to play dead, and then it is the touch of John that will bring him back to life. John will raise him up
John lowers himself down to on the floor where Branwell lays. By pressing their two bodies together, they can stand up. Once they're standing, they'll be with their feet against each other, toes against toes, knees touching, chests, together, pressing.

Branwell would play the organ for them, for their Christmas Day Service.
He could play the piano, the organ, and the flute.
There were the sad sweet notes of twenty-one airs. If it was a composer he liked, while someone else was playing the piano, Branwell would make his way through the room, with his hands swinging along in the air, hitting backs of chairs as he passed, parading in ecstasy.
The day the new organ is installed in the church it's christened by a man who's gone off to live in London. But he's come back for this one day, the special day. He is like a god, not just a man, when he plays. Branwell finds it difficult to look up, to speak, to breathe, to stir at all, while the sensation washes clean over him. And then when the music stops, only the shyest of glances is made at the man who is no longer only mortal. No mere man could make such music!
Fame, skill, knowledge, they ravish us all.
Even his body, a tall frame cloaked in black, the broad shoulders that had held all tenseness while his hands had positioned themselves, fingers loosened themselves, what to

make of it. The fairest of complexions, hair just slightly red. The ideal beauty of heroes in his writing.

Their brother sat there in the pew beside them now, watching the organ player. He held onto the pews in front of him to make his way up the aisle, up to him at the front of the church. He holds his body up straight, at the front of the church.

Was there anything he could get for him. Was there anything Branwell could assist him with. He himself might not play all that well, yet, but he was certainly an appreciative listener. In trying to talk, Branwell could only stammer a bit more along such lines of inanity, before catching himself, then regarding the fine shoes of the player. If he'd had a few drinks before coming to the church, it certainly would have been different. He'd have to walk up to Halifax sometime, and see him play some more, to see some more music.

He doesn't get to see enough music.

His sisters could play the piano. Emily was the best at that. Branwell had been to a concert or two in Leeds, and he'd found it all simply overwhelming.

As soon as he got home, he sat right down to write all about it.

It fit well into his Letters from an Englishman. He was now up to six volumes. He'd find a place for these further musings of his on music, somewhere between the wars and the banquets, the intrigues of the plays of the Kingdom of Angria. Everything was still happening in Angria.

He'd played on the organ so lovely, with such emotion.

Branwell could play in his father's church, next Sunday. He could not let himself be pulled down, just by his returning home, from London, from Bradford. The Masons, pledged to the highest moral principles, they had a piano in the space they rented for their meetings. Branwell could play on it for them, at the start or end of meetings.

He must try to forget the overwhelming.

He was also going to be appointed to Secretary of the local Temperance Society. He must agree to discount those causes of intemperance. After all, his father, the parson, was the President.

As Charlotte had, he'd help teach in Sunday School, though he'd lose his temper too often. It's something he has to watch. He's really not suited for such work. He was violently impatient with the small boys. They were only human. Branwell couldn't stand the way they just mumbled all the words, when all he wanted was a clear, right answer, when it was their turn. They'd no sense of what they were doing. They put no feeling into their reading.

One must lift one's voice to read, to God. He'd grabbed one of them by the ear, and he'd grabbed another by the shirt collar. One by the hair, and one by the arms. They must react to the words there on the page! He wants them to read to him like they are reading to God.

These young boys didn't know what he was talking about. Were they blind. They just stared at him or at the floor. They want to know what he knows. Let him try to throw them out. They were just leaving, anyway. He was an Irish, an old Irish.

*

A penniless debauchee rose from the floor of a rather sordid inn and realized this was where he'd spent the night. Still drunk, he'd had a night of revelry. He'd been around those men again whose only goal in life seemed to be to banish all traces of any remaining morality.

Branwell returned home, to write about his soldiers, heroes, visions and his versions of Byron, his romantic leads.

He'd live brilliantly on promise.

The Masons hold their meetings at the Black Bull on occasion, and Branwell is secretary of the Lodge of the Three Graces.

They drink whisky down at the Black Bull. It's the sexton, the gravedigger, John Brown, Worshipful Master, who had first taken Branwell there when he was still a boy. He could always hear the chip chip of John's mallet, as he works in the yard on headstone marbles, as the birds chirp. It's a curious thing, how the sons of parsons so often go to the bad. John Brown was nearly twice Branwell's age, though handsome. Doing his portrait, Branwell will paint him as a sensual man with an intelligent expression. Experience tests your Virgil, your virtue, your virility.

His family doesn't understand.

There, in that corner of the Black Bull, is the clock with the wood cabinet door that opens up under the glass face, inside of which the proprietor chalks up the guests' shots. Little Nosey they call him.

At the Black Bull, Branwell Brontë was a prodigy, fast becoming their own jester. The boy knows how to talk the hind leg off a donkey. Once out of the house, he makes off at once for the Bull.

There's gambling there.

There's no reason to just stand there gazing at the floor like that.

He is the one who could get any strangers passing through

the town to stay a bit longer, to spend a bit more, by keeping them so entertained with his talking, stories.

Another round!

Drinking, he no longer acted like his sisters. Branwell, the minister's son, he's the wildest boy in town!

Irish.

And more attractive than his sisters. Charlotte says so herself. Nature has been kind to him, their brother, she says, kinder to him than any of them. He's young, a dashing tough, that's how he would like to see himself. Look at how their brother can fit in. He rubs shoulders with them all, down at the Black Bull. He'd create romances on the spot, for guests passing through.

He'd try to disappear through the back door, or go out the open window in the kitchen, if one of his sisters or his father came looking for him, if it seemed he'd been a bit too long.

It's when he's not drinking that the people of Haworth laugh at him.

Outside of his family, no one takes him all too seriously. They were not so quick to jump to conclusions, but he certainly was a strange one, that Branwell Brontë. Some said it with nods, a bit more knowing than others. Some nights he'd cry to them, swearing he was going to do better, to get better. Because there's all this in him he doesn't know what to do with, something in him.

If he's had too much to drink, someone will have to carry him home.

*

No real gift for poetry at all. That's what William Wordsworth thought of Mr. Brontë. There's just silence from him, whose work Branwell has always loved. He'd sent Wordsworth a poem, much like his own Intimations of Immortality. Forgive him for this intrusion, Mr. Wordsworth. Still and bright, in twilight shining. His imitation. He's arrived at the age where he knows he must do something for himself. And he sees Wordsworth as one of the gods, along with Bryon, and Shelley, men who would never be forgotten, he believes. A thousand years to come, they'll still be remembered.

At nineteen, he writes to Wordsworth to try and place his work. He doesn't want to be forgotten either. He needed a fair judge of real poetry. He knew he couldn't just trust his sisters. He already knew youth hardened into old age, even at this age, a romantic. What he's sent was just the beginning of a much longer subject he would be undertaking and attempting to develop over his whole life.

He knows already how pressures take their toll. The passions come to collect themselves. The body bends and distorts itself under the weight, limb after limb.

He wants Wordsworth to tell him was there any point in trying to continue to write like he was trying.

All he wanted to know was if someone outside his family thought he was talented.

Since he was born, until this moment now of his writing, he'd felt he's lived hidden away, here in these hills one could hardly get to.

He doesn't know who he is, what he is, what all he might yet do.

All he is looking for is some guidance. He's read, trying to nourish himself.

Wordsworth must confess he is disgusted by the boy's conceit.

*

He's writing, at least.

Misery. Memory. Still and bright, in twilight shining.

It's time he tried the editor of Blackwood's magazine.

Believe him, he knows poetry is like a disease one must learn to live with.

He needs his letter to convey ability, pride, and independence. His cross-outs are numerous, his spellings careless. And look how dramatically his handwriting changes!

Was this boy a lunatic. They'll keep the letters, just in case. They could make for a good laugh in the future.

Sir, read what he wrote, just read it now at least.

The chief delight of his childhood, he claims, was to be found in the pages of Blackwood's, their magazine. He and his sister Charlotte and his sister Emily and his sister Anne would pore over it, read it time and again. It had helped him believe the imagination might truly be a reality. It had helped his whole childhood, he sees now, looking back as a man, to feel such a dream.

He's ready to write for them.

Tell Branwell Brontë what to write on, and he'd write on it.

The magazine must surely see they must have him, how stupid they'd be to turn him away. How could he ever write for any another but Blackwood's magazine. He's sending them a poem. All they have to do is ask for him to send more, and he will.

In the future, if they'd like, he'll send prose.

He's sending poems now because they were the easiest to read and they came most assuredly from the heart.

He's hoping their editor will have the time to let these

words enter his heart. Branwell only wants to warn them they shouldn't just write him off.

He promises to write on any subject they might like. They just have to tell him, and he'll get straight to work. Some imagination should be shown, on their part. He believes he should at least be given the chance. He's written a very lengthy, certainly—and, he believes, very remarkable—composition in prose. If they don't answer him this time, however, he promises not to write again.

So they should answer this time.

*

He must find a profession. He must choose a profession. If he's not going to be a painter, then he'll have to leave home to enter the position of private tutor, for a family in the neighboring province of Broughton-in-Furness.

It's a place he'd painted once, the district around Black Comb, four or five miles from the hill Wordsworth himself had written of a view from the summit of.

He could write while he's there, in his extra time.

His sisters have begun sewing clothes for him, stitching his collars, mending cuffs, and darning socks, in preparations for his first post as tutor.

At Broughton-in-Furness, he won't live with the family employing his services. He will lodge instead with the local surgeon. This will give him more freedom. At night, a little white house here or there dots the hills. From there, from the window, there would be just the faintest, distant glimmer of the green sea. At daybreak, how heavily he'd look out.

He'd begun to think a little bit more about his body, heart, about his chest. Of course this will never do.

Something already starts to get to Branwell, ancient ships upon ancient seas. He might hold memories in his fingers, soon. Just for now, light might plot a movement, fall of twilight, over his fingers swimming through the curtains. He'd watch the sea wasting away before him. Even it pulls back and departs for somewhere else, surging, its coursing, sliding back, heavily determined.

In writing, he believes he might hold himself. He believes he might hold an audience, if he were just given a chance. He's on the fringes of the Lake Poets' country here. He feels himself closer to them all now, all who he'd read and had been attempting to emulate ever since he was a child.

The teaching post might be suitable training for entering the Church, eventually, his father feels. If everything else failed him, his father believed, his family, there was always the Church.

But for now the Postlethwaite's sons would be his charges.

Such a clean place. The three buildings of the retired country magistrate's house sit happily alongside each other, the middle one taller, three stories up. His employer is a large landowner. On walks around the region, Branwell carries his copy of Wordsworth's sonnets.

Around this time, he and Charlotte are still discussing ideas together, still writing together. But he will work at translating Horace's Odes. He'll put them into English verse.

And she believes she's begun writing a novel, having mostly abandoned poetry. They'll have to make something of their futures.

They will have to make their way.

A year later from his post, Branwell will write. He'll write a letter to his good friend back home, John Brown.

Nobody can know he's his Worshipful Master.

Though Branwell had begun to doubt the future of his involvement with the Masons.

A riotous night in Kendal, on his way to his new post in Ulverston, off to tutor the Postlethwaite brothers. He wants to be able to tell John Brown all about such; with his lascivious, welcome bar nature. Things had to be happening first for him to have something to write to John Brown about. But John Brown would be able to understand.

Drinking was like a mask, as were the best letters.

John's his friend, his ally. He knows he has a cock and a jolly good one, too, and Branwell was not afraid to write such things. He wants these men, his friends, to hear how he could talk to them. Branwell was not all just talk. He promises they'll all have a stiffener down at the Black Bull when he comes back for the holidays. That's what he and John Brown call it.

He swears he hasn't had a drop to drink in over a year. It's hard to believe he's been there at his post for that long already. He wonders if his old friends will even recognize him anymore. And how's that old bow-legged man in the bar who's always asking Branwell about his prick, how it's standing. How was he getting along. He's just going on.

The devil would use that knob between your legs, for a walking stick, John Brown.

The last time he'd drunk was the first night he'd come to tutor these boys here. The carriage that brought him away from home had passed the school at Cowan Bridge, on the way, the place where his eldest sisters had caught their death.

But like everyone in Haworth, John Brown knows all that, surely.

A little town by the seashore, that's where he was teaching. Hills of woods rose up around him, enclosing, grasping. The boys he teaches are two fine spirited specimens, though young. And did he ever help to put their heads up in the clouds! He's taken a room from a man who drinks his weekends away, a surgeon. That doctor is a fine example. But the things he must have seen.

What did they make of him, the people here. He'd begun dressing in all black. He hadn't had a drop of whiskey to drink in over half a year, he reiterates. He swears he hasn't had a drop, not since that last time when that room at the Royal Hotel had danced before him. He'd begun the evening by playing like he was someone else. He'd begun to talk in a tone he could adopt, certain to impress them all. John Brown should have seen them. They all believed he was the life of the party, in a room that had been all lit by candles. He'd noticed the rings on all the men's fingers, men with such nice jewels. A writer notices such things.

That night it got so late men threw the contents of their glasses into each other's faces, the sides of their throats roped by the thick cords of their agitated states, all their feverish veins.

He's not afraid to say some things when he gets good and drunk enough.

There were many ways to tame a man, and men must be tamed, but John Brown knows all that. He promises not to drink again until he sees his friend.

He's been putting on a little weight, but he believes it suits him. It's a sign of good health. The old ladies who take tea in town are there to gossip with Branwell. Married, buried, devilled and damned, that's the fate of so many of the men he sees around him. He's taken to calling himself the Philosopher. He was not going to be just a tutor. But he had to keep up with his job, to approach it most soberly during the days. How he wants to believe all young girls were rightly afraid of him. He dreams of glory.

He has the use of a horse while he's there, and once he's finished giving the boys lessons, he could go to the Rose, or the King's Arms. Nobody would ever know. Except for the good Doctor, who isn't bound to discourage it. Whatever keeps a young man happy. His evenings were free.

*

Hartley Coleridge, the famous poet Coleridge's son, would prove a mighty distraction for him. He's read a translation of Hartley's of one of Horace's Odes, Hartley a poet too, and Branwell writes to him. The two of them should meet, Branwell feels. They're both poets. Branwell has sent him, Hartley, some of his own translations; and one of his very own poems, an original.

Could he visit Harltey at Ambleside.

He wants to know if he should try to continue, what Hartley might say, if Hartley might write to him. Does Hartley think Branwell should keep writing. And does he think he could ever make any money at it, with the translations he means; if he were to continue, do them all, all the books, of Horace's Odes.

From his post, Branwell has written to De Quincey, too. De Quincey, as Wordsworth's tenant, is staying in Dove Cottage.

Branwell Brontë has sent him a poem about a clock's slow ticking in the hall, weather that could threaten a group amicably gathered, a father with crippled feet, and flowers he's planted many seasons past; the old room he tries to hide his distress in, an engraving hung up of a hero in fall, a great fighting man, a man of arms. The Canadian hills embrace him, this man returning home. He wakes to see the picture of a hero that stares back at him from his wall every morning. How he wants to be him. But how could he ever be him, fallen before the charging line.

There's an elusive sorrow that stained men's sleep. The world wanted to enslave you. He assumes he speaks for most men with such sentiment. The world wanted to break one's chain of enchantment.

His home is no longer his home. Why couldn't he achieve the honors his father would have liked for him to.

Did anyone know the feeling, the feeling he has, in quite this way.

The heart ages in imperceptible ways, the splintering of degrees. That protective chrysalis, how it split.

It's this disquieting perception of the need to roam that erodes all peace.

Some of the empty husks just hang there now, men in bars.

This picture of him, this shadow of him in this poem, it means nothing to De Quincey.

*

Hartley answered him.

Branwell had been invited to spend May Day with Hartley Coleridge at his cottage at Ambleside.

Hartley was a man like him, though much older, small and frail, strange but gifted. He, too, had had an imaginary world as a child. Hartley had imagined a cataract overlying the fields, and from that milky sheen, that not quite perfect reflection, that distorting mirror, another land had grown up for him to rise off into, to escape. As a child, he could vacillate between the space of his father's friends and the world that would always mirror issuing forth from his desires.

People fall victim to self-accusation, Branwell. They are too fond of fighting, even themselves, when they felt so threatened.

They'll spend the day together, and in the future Branwell could send him some of his work. Hartley would like that. Branwell is overwhelmed.

As they walked, Branwell had the impression he is flying, as Hartley glided over the ground.

Hartley too had to watch his drinking.

There was something wanting in both of them, something they hadn't yet quite put their fingers on.

His hair, Hartley's, has gone prematurely silver white.

At Ambleside, Branwell believes he's had his first conversation with a man of real intellect; but perhaps Hartley has already forgotten him. It is a strange force that drives them to drink. Hartley had said that. The lake had been everything Branwell had imagined, everything the poets of his boyhood had told him he might find there, if he just knew where to begin looking. He's tried since childhood to make something of his life in literature. It's one of the reasons he had found himself compelled to write to the son of that famous poet Coleridge.

The lake, how beautiful the lake had been.

He knew he had to change it all in a way so everyone would be better able to understand.

All the things right for a boy of his promise to read, he had read. As of late, Branwell had been engaged with Latin, Horace and his Odes.

He was ready now, now that he'd already sown his wild oats on the page with his sisters, to begin really becoming a man.

He knew he'd have to seek real, sustained employment soon. He knew he couldn't go on like this. He had written Hartley for his expert opinion. Did Hartley see anything there in these lines of Branwell's.

When he looks at what Branwell has written him, does he.

Branwell only wants a kind word from someone like Hartley.

All he needs is a little encouragement now and then from someone who might really know something. He'll pay him to help him. They can split the money, any money Branwell might make from his translations. And if he's said anything he shouldn't have, Hartley should know it was only his inexperience talking.

A day had been spent in Ambleside. Walking side-by-side, they had been just about the same height.

In fact, Branwell was just a bit taller.

He'd send him his work, the rest, all of his translations of the Odes.

Hartley sees he's inexperienced, but he's full of ardor, too.

Look at the way he walks there alongside him, like a small pony.

It was with his father that Branwell had first read Horace, though his father wouldn't let him bring his good volume of Horace with him off to his tutoring post. He had even asked.

He waited for Hartley's words. Should he keep trying, then.

He assured Hartley he trusted him completely. He defers to his judgement. Hartley could say whatever he deems the truth, whatever he believes necessary, how much he esteems him. He could take it. Branwell could take it.

They would pay homage to each other through continued letters. Hartley had already translated some of the odes. He could recite the thirty-eighth for Branwell.

If Hartley just encourages him, Branwell will try to reach perfection, he promises that. He would retranslate everything for him. And if they were ever published, he would dedicate them to Hartley, if they were ever deemed worthy enough of the reward of printing. It would be an honor to have Hartley's name in his book.

Hartley had brought Branwell into his cottage room, where he lived all alone to devote his life to the calling of literature. And would he tell Branwell if he should in some way do the same. The blinds had been drawn, and so the room had the green hue of growing. Beech trees outside surrounded it. Ivies climbed along over the windows. He called it Nab Cottage. He places his hat up above the fireplace.

It had once been De Quincey's home.

The floor is littered with dusty papers.

If Branwell finishes his Odes, Hartley will try to help find a publisher.

Would he like some lunch. Honeydew melon.

He's a childlike man. He sleeps behind doors covered in red baize, in a bed held within white curtains.

*

After that visit, Branwell knows he must translate all of the Odes, to send them one book at a time to Hartley. He's already begun work on the first. All he has to do is finish it. He believes a drop of wine might allow him to approach the work that very evening. Those Odes are fortifying and strengthening, after work, when one is feeling a bit too sober about going on and arising the next day, to face his charges.

Not that the good Doctor, kindly old man that he was, sad widower, would get in his way, if Branwell did want to slip out for a spot of something just to warm him up, so he may contemplate what Horace might mean there in this line that could so easily shake its meaning before the eyes, before completely escaping.

He knows just the thing. There is a sacred vine outside his window, that still grows through the night, once he shuts his eyes tight, still snakes itself through sleep, syllables of Horace's mother tongue, lulling, the lullaby of Hartley having promised a new future.

Deep inside himself that feeling is only the minion of that great wine god stirring, whose voice not even his father had always been able to deny. The wine god springs at the most unexpected, surprising of times, often inopportune. Though that's part of his charm.

Branwell is to be ready for the boys tomorrow, as he listens to how the wind beats against the shutters. Calling him outside. He's a little scared, he could maybe admit to Hartley, who might understand, the feeling of being set down this deeply on one path alone in his own life, life alone in the middle of loneliness. He can't locate where exactly it lives in his body, but surely he's responsible for himself now. He should be able to take care of himself now. After all, he has two young boys entrusted to him, strong boys, too, despite their ages.

A drink was the last resort, the last resource for sleeping here.

His mind keeps turning to it so.

He has to put these feelings into words. He has to put them down strongly enough. The wine god could be all a man has out here, all alone. Look at the good Doctor.

Soon the boys would be taking their breakfast, and then waiting for Branwell.

A man's passions should be answered, that's what he'd teach.

He's seen how the Doctor gets when his bottle begins to run empty at night.

His job here now is to teach these boys, how to sing, how to chirp.

They'd be taught as he had, as well as his father had taught him. See how far Latin can take you. One day they will be able to translate Horace, just like him. Their parents only had their sons' best interests at heart. That's why Latin was so important. God's word, like the words of the gods, was written in Latin. Or Greek. And this was the service he was going to provide to them. He was going to read to them, out in the middle of this field called their place in the world.

A life of honest deeds was what they must all strive for. Horace called that singing, singing for love. Even if love one day took you far away from home.

He'd have storm clouds in his head tomorrow due to another night up late working on translations until dawn, periodically looking up at the sound like the treading of heavy boots outside the window.

No, the slouching forward of young wolves that hadn't

been taught to love. The poetry of the biting of lips, dew of the morning on leaves and hands, burying himself down deeply into his work. He knows the bed is waiting for him. But he must keep up. Something must keep him rooted here, at this desk, of his own accord, and in kind. Or why write. Why comb his hair.

He is for the grand gesture. He wants Hartley to burn these words if they disappoint; his daring, how he does, as he wrestles with duties, as he attempts to keep wrestling with everything.

In the fields around where he is posted, he hears the sound of the mares in the heat of an impending thunderstorm. The sky would soon split purple from one end to the other, revealing for a moment the lines it would soon break upon, to empty itself out.

He must return home to his assignment, soon. He has work to do.

Not just the translation of Horace's experience for Hartley, but for the boys, in the morning, too. A rosy neck, and waxen arms, the passions raised all according to Horace.

The color leaves our cheeks towards morning. But why. Why must it.

Here, he tells the boys, draw here a boy with rosy cheeks, like yourselves.

He has work to do. If the drawing is good enough, he'll reward them with a bit of his Horace.

Yes, Horace. H-O-R-A-C-E, not horse. An important poet.

No, not hoarse either, like you'll be after he gets through with you if you don't bend down over that drawing.

Let's see who can be the first person to say nothing.

He hears the falter in his tone. He should have slept more last night. Or had a bit more to drink. Two boys just stare at him, uncomprehendingly. Horace doesn't stir them, though he wants it to. Even boys should be stirred. But he might as well be reading the Bible to them.

Bring me the whip from your father's stable, and then class is dismissed for the day. Then they can do whatever they want to. They must simply stay out of Branwell's way, and don't let their parents see them, either.

He could no longer evaluate what he's written.

He needs Hartley's opinion, his further guidance on this. He needs another set of wise eyes. He was going blind at night, trying to copy the words out to the candle, to keep them neat enough to read, himself lucid enough to continue on with any sense of the next line, while the flame gutters.

In his room he's translating a formal knowledge of great models before his charges. The Odes are wine-soaked. At night he returns to his lonely task.

But all great minds must leave melancholy thoughts behind.

White shoulders stained with wine. In wine, he'd forget, he'd try to forget, this mounting misery here; forget in wine that provoked song, in wine that creates life, in wine that sustains his work.

He wants Hartley to tell him yes, he should be in a better place, he should be better employed, or what was the use in further cultivating charms he feels might be wasted, until he is absolutely sure.

A man must bear his lot in patience, his father would tell him.

In the morning he wouldn't feel like waking, walking, moving a foot from bed. He wants to dream more of the odes he is going to finish one day for Hartley. But the boys, those two little bright-eyed things, must be faced. He'd use that whip on them, if they didn't mind him, if they didn't just keep quiet. They must be shown what's right, the proper path. It's the only thing he's been brought here to do. Nothing more, after all. They didn't have to love their lessons, but youth without love was wild and rude, uncultivated, uncontrollable, so saith Horace. Only out of the suffering of discipline poetry might come.

Hartley must be able to sense Branwell's thrown himself upon the mercy of the word, thrown his fate to the gods to deal with him.

*

After that day with Hartley, convinced he was going to be somebody else, Branwell had become a bit careless in his position as tutor, it must be admitted. He'd frequently find himself walking in the countryside, making his way to the nearest bar.

He's left the boys with some pictures of his own he'd like them to come up a story for, a long one. Or he could tell them a story about it tomorrow, if they hadn't managed to come up with anything today. They could all make up a story together. It's how you made your way in the world. And if they were to finish that, then they should begin on their own sketches.

They could put away their math books now.

There might be some use eventually for their Greek, but not today.

He'd begun to dream in wayside inns.

There's the Sun Hotel, the Queen's. He'd return home drunk with everything Hartley had said to him.

He wants his father to get him out of this, this whole teaching, tutoring position.

If he could come home, home to Haworth, he could finish his translations more quickly, and then he could be someone more quickly. But he couldn't tell his father that. Not those words, exactly.

He couldn't bear being away from home. Just like Emily. He was becoming sick with the need for some familiarity. Like Charlotte. They were exploiting him in his position, they were degrading his father's only son. His health was failing, to the point that yesterday he'd believed he'd seen a wolf circling him, coming up behind him, knowing, when he was just trying to walk home.

Before his father can call him back home, though, Mr. Postlethwaite finds Branwell in a delicate state he'd never want to see any tutor of his sons in. He's been keeping his eye on him, on the example he might be setting for his sons. He knows Branwell has been meeting these poet chaps in outlying bars. He'd sent someone out looking for him, when Branwell wasn't where Branwell was supposed to be. That's when he'd been disgracefully discovered, with some supposed poet friend he claims he knows from Leeds.

They'd only been for a ride in his friend's carriage, then stopped off at the bar to rest the horse. But Mr. Postlethwaite wants Branwell to take his things and go.

His sisters would understand, they would know how these families could be, all they expect for so little, that sickness growing inside you, that gnawing, wanting to get back home. You were more a servant than a teacher.

Charlotte has decided to send a letter to Hartley Coleridge, too, about her own work, because she knows what their brother has been up to, how he's been asserting himself outside them. She has been working now in prose.

But Hartley wouldn't flatter her back.

She's glad for the critique, though, she tells him in her return letter. She could tell he's an honest man. Just like his father. And a gentleman, to have even replied to her.

She could stop what she was writing then and try something else. He was kind to give her this direction. It was just the beginning of something that would have been too long. But surely he must know what it's like to want to be a part of society.

Perhaps her heroes really are for nothing more than a Lady's magazine, perennially flourishing. She can't remember now if it had been her mother's or her aunt's that she'd once read. It was so long ago. One day, their father had burned every last one of them, because of the bad examples they set with their love stories. They were all stained by the water of the sea.

Such dreams. But she hadn't told him she was Branwell Brontë's sister, had she. She may write like a lady, but whatever did that mean, really. Dickens, Richardson, and Rousseau to her all write like women at times, too! Of course she's only being demi-serious, she writes. You see, her C could be for Charles or Charlotte, and what did he think the T for the last name place might stand for.

Hartley was going to write her brother back, but it's a letter never sent, never finished completely. Just a draft. He's not unkind, and he hasn't forgotten Branwell, but he's just been looking all this time for the right words. There's only ever been one young man he's found obviously so full of merit. Branwell. He must have told him, or he must know, he must have felt, all he'd made Hartley respond to there in his lines, real life coiled in those words he'd chosen, words like taut gloves over the feelings.

He didn't think Branwell should publish the whole of his Horace, but some of his Odes are quite fine, and they could appear with very little alteration.

It was a pleasure to see him. A pleasure. There was so much promise in him.

He'd like to commend Branwell a bit more on the way he had attempted to take that something untranslatable in Horace, into English, those effusions of youth, all that Horace must have been thinking. Branwell shows a command of a number of things. Hartley was impressed with Branwell's search for an English potentially racy within such confines, he writes in the letter never sent.

Branwell will never hear from him again.

*

He returned from the teaching post, like when his studio hadn't been a success and he'd gotten into a bit of debt. His father wanted him back there. There was nowhere else for him to go but back.

He'd left Bradford in the middle of a painting, one the varnish had not yet been applied to. Somebody else would have to complete such minor details for Branwell, sweep up the loose ends after him. He doesn't have money to go back to Bradford, just to finish a portrait of his landlord and landlady. Somebody would have to be kind enough to pay his overdue rent there, too.

The unfinished portraits were meant to cover a month or two's rent.

In Bradford, he'd worn his top hat at an angle, pale gray trousers, carried a fashionable cane. At Ambleside, he'd become friends with Coleridge's own son. And a poet named James. He wants everyone in Haworth to know what James had seen in him, how much James had liked him. James had launched the Bradford Philosophical Society, with six talks on English poets. He'd told James that he wanted to be a poet, had confided this to him, and James had done nothing but encourage him. He should keep trying. A poet lived from day to day.

Their father wanted him to come back home, to find something he could do right there in Haworth. There was no more money to give Branwell. His children were going to have to learn to support themselves. They would not be able to live off of what they'd be left when he died one day. They would not last for long.

And what had Branwell done in Bradford, really. He'd drunk, drunk because he knew he was supposed to be somebody. Why would he ever want to go back there. All he'd done in Bradford was spend his days in the studios of other men, or in the bars of hotels, watching while others worked.

He'd painted portraits, some, but he was not making his way in the world, not yet. He'd conducted himself perfectly properly in the room where he'd lodged, in Bradford, and in Broughton-in-Furness, he says. They'd liked him. He'd been a steady young gentleman in their eyes in Bradford. They have nothing but kindness to report back about him.

Patrick Brontë didn't want his only son succumbing to vice. He wanted him to be nothing but someone he'd be able to be proud of.

Branwell could turn one of the rooms upstairs into a studio, if he doesn't like the old peat closet anymore, if he feels it is too small for his work. He could paint at home. Why did one think he had to be in some place like Bradford. He could paint right here.

Charlotte, home for a break from a tutoring post, has tried not to laugh when their brother mentions this time the Kingdom of Angria. She's more interested, now that she's seen the world, in what she likes to call the human emotions, real human nature.

She is learning French, as one has to if one wants to teach quality young girls. In Brussels, Monsieur Heger would help her perfect her rudimentary understanding of it. Both Charlotte and Emily would go to Brussels; and if Emily doesn't want to stay, Anne could always take her place.

Of course, Monsieur Heger is a fine example, a worldly, worthy, married man.

A woman was to give her life for a man, and Charlotte believes a man should be prepared to do the same.

Branwell, isn't that right.

But Branwell has some poems to show their father's new curate, Mr. William Weightman.

Who is always over at the house these days.

Did William want to see Branwell's Horace translations.

Would William write to him when he goes away for a few days, to pass his final ordination examinations before returning to Haworth.

Yes, William will write him long letters, of all the ladies he'd find to fall in love with, at all the balls he'd also be attending while away.

Men like him and William could share such things between themselves.

Surely his sisters had noticed all of William's strengths, too, his strong character.

William understands Branwell. They are two gentlemen both in the bloom of youth, one of them on the verge of becoming the new curate. Something must be done with that youth of theirs. Like men, he and their brother would discuss ideas of hearts and souls among themselves, become as brothers.

What attracted one to another would be difficult to say.

*

There's no one to talk to about this, the condition of his soul, his accumulating debts, debts that would follow him throughout his life, if his life was to be one of drinking. The things their brother had seen in the streets, that August, when he'd visited Liverpool. Their sister Charlotte was off at her school. The world was to be a bigger world for her. And Anne had begun following her lead.

They do come home to visit, though. William the curate is around more often than required.

He could be a love interest, for their sister Anne!

Charlotte likes to believe herself just simply amused by such things.

Look at the way Anne lights up when William enters the room, the way she quickly looks down. Could Branwell believe there was such a blush to her cheeks. William had firmly entered the picture of their parsonage. He was going to establish a parochial and lending library, for all the good people of Haworth. At times he looked so delicate, pale. But unlike Branwell, he was interested in the church. He was too young to be a curate!

He's almost a brother to Branwell. He's only twenty-five. Miss Celia Amelia, his sisters jokingly call William. But it's not a joke to Branwell. He'll write an Amelia poem, how she, Amelia, beguiles the speaker who knows Amelia must feel like him. They must have the same feelings.

William is distinctly handsome in a somewhat feminine style. He could be so dainty. He has sun-colored curls. His eyes are blue. And look at his lips. Branwell notices his lips. His cheeks are so pink.

He is just down from university. He's just left university. He'll show Charlotte his university gown.

Look, she could feel it. That's what pure silk felt like. What did she think.

Look how Anne will be shy around him. Why, there's no need. He's the lightest heart she'll ever know, the kindest. Through and through, he is simply a male flirt. Emily doesn't want him there, in the house, not at first, and he'd taken to calling her the Major!

Charlotte finds it all so terribly exciting.

Why doesn't he let Charlotte advise him about his love affairs.

Miss Weightman, Branwell's sisters all call him, and he just blushes.

They will all be friends, their hearts leaping up around the fire. That's how one of them was going to describe it. He'd call him his dearest friend, William. It seems their brother's affections are given almost entirely to men. He can write to him. William will cheer him up.

But watch how the curate makes animal eyes at Anne, as they are all sitting in church. They are supposed to be listening to the sermon! He'll send them all valentines, each and every one of them, since they've foolishly told him how they've never received a single valentine before among them.

Amorous verses fill them.

Surely William Weightman was not made to be a curate.

Even among themselves, they could hardly believe it. Such simple things simply did not happen in Angria, in Gondal. Blue eyes, auburn hair, and his rosy cheeks.

He and Branwell were going to hunt grouse together, snipe or heathcock.

They were going to go out with the guns.

William's arm is so strong as he holds onto the butt of the gun, swings it along in his hands. He handles it well.

Then sometimes they'd go back to William's room together, and share a bottle of the flat beer he has in his room. This is the companionship their brother has so badly needed.

Charlotte says she knows he has faults; put in his position who wouldn't, but she will defend William to her dying day. A whirlwind friendship, and whenever he's away, they're sure to all correspond regularly.

*

At twenty-three, their brother opts for the more manual labor of employment on the new Leeds and Manchester railway that has just opened. It was something he could do until his literary career took off. He has a number of connections already to the business. He's painted the portrait of a man who can perhaps get him a job on the line. And there are men he knows from the bars in Bradford who could put in a good word for him.

He'll be offered the job of Assistant Clerk in Charge at Sowerby Bridge Railway Station. It would be a fresh start, a new post. He feels the need to make this new job sound like something, to believe it might be, because, at this time, according to Charlotte, what had he accomplished.

Some days his voice still has a ringing sweetness. His sisters still dream they can eventually open a school together somewhere, if not in Haworth, then somewhere where their brother and father and aunt could all come visit them.

It's Charlotte's dream.

Emily doesn't say anything, when Charlotte goes on like this with all her plans.

Anne, she's game. She's game for whatever Charlotte would like.

Emily's going out for a walk.

Charlotte says they can talk about the school later. You see, it would be so much better if all of them could do it together. Wouldn't Emily join in.

It's after the railroad that things will never be the same. Sowerby Bridge, where he becomes a railway clerk, is close to Halifax, closer to home than his teaching post.

The Railway Bridge lies at the center of town.

It is expensive to drink. And then there are the other things he sometimes does, the opium. He looks at De Quincey, and his Confessions of an English Opium Eater, and all the poetry it opened up for him.

He doesn't want it to become too much of a habit.

He could be doing something much better than this, if he wanted. It appears to the people he talks to on and around the railroad that he uses English perfectly, like a young gentleman. Charlotte finds it hard to believe this is the life he'd choose for himself.

Ah, he'd be in excellent spirits, to be away from home, embarking on his new adventure. He will stay at Sowerby Bridge this year for Christmas. He can tell all of them at the parsonage he has too much work to do. He can not get away. Though Emily and Charlotte are soon to take off for Brussels, and he might not see them for a good long while.

They are all going to learn to be schoolteachers.

This was a job he'd have to keep this time. Is he sure this is what he wants.

Everything raises an echo there in the station. The offices smell of the green woods, the roof of the station a corrugated metal the rain hits against.

The railroads tunnel through the mountains.

He lodges in an old house with wooden shutters. The arched doorway of the building, situated on a hill, overlooks the railroad station just down below. Downstairs they sell beer, and there are even more places to get it up in the village.

He brushes his red hair up after walking through the steam, the train's exhaust, the rain at night.

Has anyone ever told him he has a roman nose.

There at Sowerby, he'll be closer to the culture and arts that both Halifax and Bradford have to offer. Halifax is just two and a half miles, uphill. He still has friends. The men he'd met in Bradford often go there. There's the heat of discussion. There's his sculptor friend Leyland.

Leyland, he has a way of looking at him. Don't look at him like that, Leyland. He had work to get back to. He was handsome in his checked coat. His vest had a line of brocade running in it. Feel it, Branwell. His black cravat knots nicely at his neck. He's one of his closest friends, doesn't he know that.

Afterwards, in winter, the cold road feels iron hitting hard up under his thin worn work shoes.

Woolven has gotten him the job, though his only real references were his father and his aunt. The proprietor of the Black Bull won't count. Branwell had been watching the construction of the railway for quite some time. They told him how it was going to change everything. He'd become quite a popular figure with the men working up and down the line. You would be able to go by train from one end of the country to the next one day. Mark their words. The power of that engine, the hissing of that steam, those trains like snakes, snaking the countryside, spraying soot, their black clouds, all the men employed to make this happen, the talk of it, how it would happen one day, all through their labors, their need to work only, sealing it for Branwell.

They are all coarse men, rowdy and rough, Charlotte guesses.

These are not the type of men their father would want to see his son with, but look at their builds. He could draw them, sketch them working. They work with their hands. From sketches he's made, he can then paint them, their hands creased with earth. Some of them live on the barges, moored up around developing tracks, running along the waterways. They are an anonymous band of people, gypsies.

*

Branwell is scared of girls. He says of Charlotte's friend Mary Taylor that she's too pretty to live. She might have expected something more from him than admiration from afar.

Months and months away from home, what will he do with himself.

Mary Taylor believed she was the kind of woman who might make a worthy mate out of a man like Branwell Brontë. She'd want some real proof of his love though. Charlotte believes Mary had made the fatal mistake of showing herself too easy a conquest, too simple and straightforward.

A boy like Branwell had to be captured in a more roundabout way.

The way he'd captured Mary's imagination, as she played the piano. He'd laughed and sung along.

Mary doesn't want only to show off her dress, she wants to talk about the bread shortage. Her family's house is made of bricks. Imagine, Branwell! It is red!

But there'd be no flowering of a stock romance here, while his sisters looked on. Now Mary wondered if she'd ever marry, Charlotte confides in a letter to another friend, pleased with the ring of the muse inside her, the pleasure just the sound of it brings.

Charlotte could see herself being treated the way her brother had treated her friend Mary Taylor, who had wanted nothing but to one day marry him. Their brother won't listen to reason. He was going to be a railway clerk.

She can't see how he'll ever imagine himself a knight in such a position. But he seems to believe there's adventure to be had there.

After three months of ticket-taking, he's transferred to another station. In less than a year, a promotion to Luddenden Foot where as Clerk in Charge he'll be given more money. Man thinks too often, he has decided in a poem, words for a Lord of his to speak. He's still writing on the railroad.

It looks like getting on at least to Charlotte, the transfer up the line, to a station a little more out of the way, a little less lively, a little more isolated. He'll have a co-worker, more free time, time to himself, the trains not coming through quite so often, a mile or so up the line from Sowerby. He won't be out there all alone. There are musical concerts in Halifax he can attend, and he can ride the train for free now.

Luddenden Foot is known locally as Little Switzerland.

At the station, he'll sketch in a notebook, his job to collect tickets and keep books. He's twenty-four. The warmth and joy of this period comes from being around the machines. Affections must remain friendships.

He'll search for signs, tokens in other people's eyes.

He'll write to William. Charlotte is sure William must be interested in at least one of them. Anne seems most taken by him, if one's to believe the poems she writes are about him.

The whole station itself was nothing but a wooden hut in a clearing. It's just him and a porter, the wooden platforms. Some nights he believes he's felt the voice of his sister, Maria, out there when walking or looking for the train.

He's cut off, unless he wants to get on the train, and take it into where they drink. Occasionally his friend, Grundy, comes to visit him. When side by side, in twilight, sitting, Branwell writes.

They'll go to one of the bars where his spirits could rise. A draft cuts through the hut, in winter. Down into his bones, it makes its way. This wretched coldness, a parching thirst, sickly loathing, and the overwhelming confusion of shame.

Grundy shares a room with a double bed with another

man who works around those parts. Grundy was finally getting away from his widowed mother, calls his arrangement with the other man chumming-in. There was something innately vulgar about his friend Grundy.

Branwell writes poems, draws the outlines of his own face, his own profile.

There are fewer passengers, fewer trains, longer pauses between them. But they shake through, when they do come, the smoke griming the dull windows of the hut station.

He'd write the names of the men he met out there in his notebook in Greek letters.

His conduct, he feels, is marked by a cold debauchery, cutting its way down into his soul. There's the Lord Nelson to drink at, which stood in a square about a mile or so uphill from the station, beside the church.

He's chipping away at what he once dreamed of being.

For just these nights, they exchange their lives, from the distance over drink. He likes the places where the rough types and cultivated gentlemen meet. He's lost there everything familiar, but drink, his constant companion.

Just how far could he push this body.

His figure is slim, agile, formed well. The men he finds himself around help him size himself up. His complexion was clear. There was something benevolent, still in him, the expression on his face could be so cheerful, even here.

Wollsom, was he a wollsom boy. They joked in their accents. Hard-heeled manufacturers who hadn't heard him speak yet eyed him. The flash in his eyes would cast down around their work boots, at the Red Lion, the Shuttle and Anchor.

He's afraid he might have been born with an evil nature,

as something in the humid darkness he believes was growing in him.

Books in parlours of some bars smell of malt and grain.

If life is intolerable, what could he do to alter it.

He never removed his glasses. He talked to the men who manned the barges, down around the water, outside the bars. Desperately lonely, he walked out to seek, find. He was just out for a walk, while the traffic of coal and wool passed through the train through the station.

He pushed his body down the road, up the hill.

There was a book he'd heard about, concerning the causes of the premature decline of one's manhood. He made a note of it. He'd always carry a little notebook with him.

He was surrounded by reckless soldiers, wanted for desertion, drunks, their murdering of all authority.

He doesn't want to be left alone, as the railroad goes so silent late at night.

How might immortality be achieved, despite poverty, a low birth, any number of adversities. There had been other parsonage children who had lost their mothers at an early age. There had been men in Branwell's position before, men who had gone on in the past to achieve greatness. Great men, those should be the subjects of his poems. He makes a list of fourteen of these heroes to worship.

He'll write in his railway notebook, back at Haworth, when he leaves this post after eighteen months.

It's his writing of heroes Charlotte may find, while looking through the drawers of the house, that habit she had. She wanted to know where everything was.

The word Jesus recurs many times in Branwell's notebook. He called his disciples the sons of thunder. Branwell writes the word Jesus next to the names of other men. There had been many hours in Luddenden to explore the countryside with men he'd met, like a sacred music. The manufacturers of the town all knew him by sight. He knew how to write all of their names in Greek. Or let him draw you. He'd sketch one in a chair reclining back.

He'd do it full-length, that way he could draw the crossing of the legs, with a tall hat on one's head, back up against the high-back of the chair, not just one man. A number of men Branwell combined in the drawing, to pull them all together, to try to imbue one with the quality of timelessness; this type that would always be around. Some of them, laborers, had let their hair go long, men whose wives had died. One was a young man recently wealthy. One was recently widowed. One was a man who could hold out his hand to one who might need it. There was a great power in being able to do such.

They believe Branwell has been taking money that's gone missing from Luddenden Foot. Someone, their father, will have to make up the difference.

Their brother has been dismissed for constant carelessness, books just not adding up. Money has been allowed to go untracked. Somehow it has slipped right through his hands. Or he's been drinking with it.

His negligence has allowed for it to be misplaced in any case.

His job was to run a tight ship, and they'd expected him to have the accounts prepared properly.

His family can't know.

No, he'll tell them he's taken sick, that is why he has had to come back home again.

It's not all that serious, the offense. Other men had through their negligence caused a number of crashes, trains to derail. When sections of track were taken up, men would sometimes forget to fly the red flag. Men would go drinking, and then they'd go to drive down the tracks, and another crash could have easily happened.

He hasn't been sentenced to hard labor, not like some of the others would be.

He's filled in the margins of the books he was supposed to be keeping with his writings and drawings. He'd often left the ticket office for the porter to mind, while going off to drink, looking for someone else to talk to other than just that porter.

Sometimes these absences would last for days.

The village itself was only an inn and a few houses, but there were farms lying around the station with open doors. It was a nice neighborhood to go wandering in, to get lost and drunk in.

He roamed the hills afterwards, laughing, running, Sodom, leaving his lot. It took him six glasses now to feel anything.

Red sparks, cigars, lit up the dark. Men smoked here and there along the road. He'd quickly walk down the dark lanes, breathing hard, nails marking into the palms of his hands balled up into fists shoved down deep into the pockets of his coat. He'd wanted to try to get away from home. He'd return to Haworth weekends by hiring a gig to take him there. At least one of his sisters would likely be there.

He is not shy, unlike his sisters.

He'll talk to strangers. He'd meet men on the road, walking, become friends with them. They would challenge him to a wrestle, right then and there. They were weavers and factory hands, merchants, owners of mills, all sorts of men. Around those parts, once he'd been let go by the railroad, they'd come together, write letters for Branwell, petition for him to be given his job back.

Wouldn't they let him come back to his post, once he'd gotten better.

Why was he crying now.

He wanted to be around those he could impress. He wanted to be flattered, to be believed to be someone.

His family, they didn't understand.

It couldn't be that even simple clerical work was beyond him.

He's just a boy.

He must be punished.

He leaves the house towards the Black Bull. Leave him alone, let him go.

He's been driven further to the bad, Charlotte believes.

He is a brilliant conversationalist, the way he'd held all the workers in thrall, made friends with engineers, entertaining them, on lines that still came close by Haworth.

He is to take more opium, like Coleridge, De Quincey, to live, to paint.

It will reveal things to him. It will reveal life. It will create a mist for him to walk in. It will keep him strong, protect him.

If someone could just put in a good word for him. Could there be another post, another appointment, possibly at the railway. He's too short to be a soldier. Won't go into his father's Church. That much is certain. They're all hypocrites, he says boldly in a letter to a friend from the area.

At times a coarseness had begun to slip out into his speech, at home, one of the things he would have to learn to try to control. He'd rise up again, he writes to his friends, sketching in one or two of the half-buried tombstones he sees from his window.

*

A bird singing a certain way announced desire to Emily. She sees the animals picked off one by one, nowhere left to go where they are not exposed. There had been no mother to care for any of them.

Their brother hadn't changed yet. He was like the caterpillar, still taking in everything, pulling it into himself, chewing it, to create what might be silk for the cocoon, eventual fulfillment. She feels it within her power to hurt those around, but she won't. She'll dream for him on a bench in a park in Brussels, when she's there with Charlotte. She'll dream of wings too small to spot, not yet touched, and the sky one large wing all over them. One day, pulled back, what it had been shielding them from would be revealed.

Perhaps they would see more clearly then.

Their brother is the only one home when William, their curate, dies. He'd die in his arms. Already at this young age, William is dying. It is cholera. Branwell had nursed him.

He had admired and loved Branwell. Even more than most of his friends. That's what they all must see now.

It would break your heart, to think about him, only twenty-eight. There are two weeks of vomiting, dysentery, a fever that climbed up into his final delirium.

First William Weightman dies, then their aunt follows, two deaths separated by a mere one or two weeks.

Charlotte and Emily were off in Brussels, and Anne was at her post at Thorp Green. Branwell stood by the young man's bedside. He walked over to the window, then came over closer to the bed when he called to him.

It was only year three of his curacy. Branwell was the only one there to hear their father deliver the funeral service for William. They had all been pleased to make his acquaintance, honored. He calls William one of his dearest friends.

But he's left them now, gone.

William had left them. There was no hope for Anne now, as his stone was placed outside of the Old Haworth Church. They'd all loved him. Anne had found him so kind. He'd been something in their brother's life, to have back in Haworth. How he'd enlivened them all for a time. In flights of words Anne fancied a departed, fair angel, insisting to herself the soul of man was divine.

Now Branwell was afraid he felt the brush of death's wings every day.

His father has nothing but praise for the great man William had been. He breaks down. Branwell sits in the family pew, where he never would during the teaching of Sunday school. Branwell had liked to be close to the window, to read in secret by the sun.

He's there alone, all his sisters still away, their aunt at home dying, even as William's funeral service was taking place.

His father says William had been like a son to him. William had never understood why people should want to create for themselves artificial sorrows. Sadness disturbed praise. It had been natural for them all to be taken by

William, his presence a pleasure, not a constant burden. William was temperate, benevolent, a success, respected.

On this vain, selfish, bustling world, he's now closed his eyes.

Their father reads on in a sermon his parishioners will all want published later. Branwell could not control the way his body then seized in a buckle, as he began to cry loudly, to buck in the pew. He doesn't ask for William, as he'd asked aloud for Maria, to speak to him.

Now he knows it is too late.

That was so long ago, seventeen years ago.

He tries to choke back down inside himself feeling, as they wonder around him if he's drunk, or worse, carrying on in such a way in the church at a funeral. They carry out the body to the churchyard.

They'll bury William where they'll one day bury Branwell.

*

Their aunt, Miss Branwell, their mother's sister, used the word tawny to describe Branwell's hair. She'd said they were all holy, all filled with Grace. But he doesn't feel this. Why doesn't he. Why can't he.

Her lips had pinched in in a smile.

She'd tried to convince him time and again he was one of the saved, but he doesn't feel it. He believes he may be irredeemably damned. He's terrified of what they say is bound to happen to him, if he keeps carrying on, drinking the way he has.

He writes a friend that for two nights he'd watched his aunt trying to die.

Her teapot was still there on the table. To live is a gift.

To live is thrift. The script runs round it. To die, she's been waiting for days to die. Finally gain grace.

He was the only one of the children who'd been attached to her in any way, and he was there, there the whole time, for two weeks, watching over her, as he'd watched over William. He fears he's becoming incoherent through the succession of deaths.

Sorrow made it hard for him to see.

Their aunt, she was connected to all the happy times of his childhood, he writes. And now she dies. She'd given him money. He tells everyone how for twenty years she'd been like his mother, indulging him in a way she hadn't the girls.

Death will not quit.

They take their toll.

Youth is spent and lost quickly.

How quickly things are taken away.

She'd hated this landscape of bleak winter. In her will, she'd leave to him the most masculine of her possessions, a lacquered dressing box from Japan. He could keep things in it. Like the small gold box from her bedroom she'd once taken her snuff out of.

He'd disappointed her. He knows he had. With so many talents, though, she must have believed, he will one day be able to prosper in earning his own living.

After this, he must try to stay sober, remain sensible.

*

He is around twenty-five when he first comes to Thorp Green, where his sister Anne has been for some time, and with her good word, has secured him a post.

As if he were still Captain of something, Anne will watch

the way their brother leads his new young charge around, embarking on some grand adventure. Anne will watch them through manor windows.

It's an isolated hamlet, even more cut off than their moors of Haworth. It's an estate, between Ripon and York. The district is finely wooded, fertile, made up of various manors and farms.

Entrance Hall, Dining Room, Drawing Room, Library, Breakfast Room, Kitchen, Servants' Hall, Cellar, eight Lodging Rooms on the first floor, nine on the second floor.

Their bedstead was from France.

The carpet in the drawing room was from Brussels.

Ah, Brussels. A piano!

They hear he plays.

Fine oil paintings on all their walls. He was to bring their son up to such a standard, if their son was to ever be an artist of any worth.

Four or five servants room at the top of the house. They are summoned for by little bells. Then there are the grooms, out in the stables, where their collection of horses are kept.

Such a big building takes your breath away!

It's a splendid place with red carpet throughout, the chairs covered in a matching red. The tables are draped with matching cloths. The fresh white ceiling is trimmed around in gold.

A silver and glass chandelier spills its light all from the center.

Her brother smiles at the furniture. The clock, gold, too, ticks.

Outside, it's like Paradise, like where he took their sister Charlotte once when he was fifteen, and she, sixteen, visiting a friend. The lawns are a velvet green. Green fields, chestnut trees on the lawn, battlements, a rookery, orchards and gardens of fruit trees.

There in Thorp Green, the cream and butter come from their own dairy.

They make their own beer in the Brew-house.

That outbuilding is a Wash-house.

Surely he will come to value his time here.

There were the stables, surrounded by Irish rose.

The Robinsons of Thorp Green own fourteen horses.

He'd had no references, only his sister, Anne.

There's the Coach-house, the Saddle Room.

The husband, Mr. Robinson, was more often gone with the hounds than at home.

His sister Anne is already settled there, already valued there, has been for quite some time. She'd noticed that one of her pupils seemed abnormally drawn to the stables, the stable-lads, the grooms, as was the boy at times.

They'd be valued here, both he and Anne, Anne just knows it, in this other home, their new home, where they've rejoined each other.

Large windows in the front of the house extend to the ground, open out onto the lawns. But he won't live there in the Hall, not in the main house, not like Anne. Branwell will live in the building they affectionately call Monk's House. Or some still called it Old Hall.

That first night, that first week, that first month or so there's homesickness. Even though Anne is close by, up in the main house.

He could sketch Monk's House, with its long chimneys,

steeply pitched roof, the stretch of its rough bare walls barely relieved by windows. A seventeenth-century red brick house with a Dutch-style roof, it is part of the farm, out closer towards the stables. He's going to sketch the building from the back, for a better view. A tree cuts across its stone, in his foregrounded perspective.

Even this outer building alone is bigger than their house back home.

He could sketch the lodgings, when not sketching the men with guns who went for game around the grounds.

The grounds of Thorp Green were flush.

Branwell's charge, Edmund, may come daily to Monk's House for lessons. It will make for a change from the little schoolroom where Anne still has lessons with the daughters not yet married.

At first, Edmund tries to hide in the folds of the brown curtains, to avoid any further instruction. As if Branwell could not see his form behind there, the black shoes peeking out.

Maybe this way Anne can keep her brother away from the Black Bull. It was not as easy to get to those friends who encouraged him from here. And Branwell has to do something. He himself has said he'd rather lose his hand, than experience again that loss of himself out on the railway post, his real worth, ever again.

Branwell had a natural gallantry. How could any member of the Robinson family not see that. They'd taken him into their fold. A great writer must regret past mistakes. He was penitent, in his words.

Their brother would be the perfect tutor for the

Robinsons' son. He was to learn Latin. The Robinsons want to send the boy off to a public school eventually, but he just can't seem to learn the bare basics he'll need in order to get on there with the others. He is soon to be eleven years old. He is their only son, the mother's especial favorite. Branwell has been hired for him alone.

As teachers, he and Anne are there to teach only approved things.

Now he will be there with her. Now Anne won't be so lonely.

Anne had tried to teach the boy, but at ten he couldn't read the simplest line in the easiest book. Like a horse neighing, he stutters over them, whinnying. He hangs his head, eventually to one side.

As if he were trying to break from the yoke of letters.

She had been trying to teach him for a good two years. It will be a pleasant change for her now to concentrate on only the sisters.

He must be mild and patient. The boy is so nervous, skittish, whenever the notion takes him to be, a small boy, a pale boy, with the image of his mother visibly stamped upon his features. He's to keep his temper with the boy. Branwell doesn't find him all that hard to approach.

*

He slinks around his mother's feet. Keep the boy happy. He, Young Master Edmund, is accustomed to only the best, the most tender treatment.

He's a darling.

Surely Branwell, like she, feels how they are another thing altogether, all alone here surrounded by such creatures as the

Robinsons, with their fine dresses, and fine dishes. Look at the china patterns! These are Passages in the Life of an Individual, Anne has begun writing. They were strangers to such comforts as those they had here.

The boy was still all green around the edges, all impressionable youth.

He and Branwell were going to sketch species of birds. There were so many around the grounds of Thorp Green, with so many wooded areas. They could find them hiding there.

Now if only Branwell could trade this brush, this pen, for his hunting gun. Does Young Edmund know how to shoot. Anne had warned him. He should watch out for the boy, the boy could be pettish, cowardly, selfish. He seems to like nothing better than to get into trouble, this boy surrounded by women. He's good at making up lies. He even does it out of some malevolent joy.

Branwell has taken a pen name for his poetry. He calls himself Northangerland, and he'd like the boy to use it when referring to him, too, that character he'd first written about long ago with Charlotte, during the Angrian chronicles of their childhood.

He is far from all he once knew. The boy would be his concern, what he will teach him tomorrow. Edmund must learn to trust him, to come closer, out of his corner. Soon he'll have him eating out of his hand. He'll give him a little lump of sugar.

Though she's been offered a position of much higher pay in England, though actually making much less than even

Branwell himself during his days on the railway, though in fact losing money, Charlotte is to stay on in Brussels.

She writes a letter home to their father asking him to please let her stay, there with her Master Heger.

Branwell would curl his hair. He would scent his handkerchiefs.

There at home at the Black Bull, they'd have trouble recognizing him at Thorp Green!

She had a taste for a certain strain of poetry, too, this Mrs. Robinson, the lady of the house. She recognized that artistic streak in Anne and her brother, recognized how perfect they'd be for the mannered education of her children.

Branwell was like a new member of the family.

Look at all she was able to give him, and would.

Their sister Charlotte writes to him now in the words of Angria, their Angria she knows she should feel guilty about revisiting when there's M. Heger, Brussels, the real world. All alone, late at night, in her room, thoughts turn back to the kingdom of their childhood. Charlotte shouldn't think such thoughts, she knows. But she does.

Through her childhood imagination, M. Heger could become everything to her, her Black Swan. She writes it with the capitals, in letters home to Emily, Emily who'd left Brussels, Emily who didn't want to be a teacher ever.

Emily will now keep the sandstone of the hall floor and the stairs clean. Since there is no paper on the walls, the dove-color that tints them can be more thoroughly washed. Haworth is the place of welcoming shadows. They welcome Emily back home. And one day they will welcome Branwell back, too.

In Haworth, one attempted to remain merely one step

ahead. It had been easy for them all in Haworth, but now they needed to exercise their intelligence a bit more. Charlotte knows that once home Emily will have her hands full with their father, who ails a bit more each day, sees less and less the faces that come before him. Emily says in writing he could just see his way up the stairs, but still insists on climbing them. He still takes his meals alone, his eyes filming as he stares in front of him.

A man of his temperament, only the Greeks, the Romans, would understand. Those men were all now gone to dust.

There in Haworth, Branwell had gone almost mad, with nothing to listen to but how the sky blew over the ash trees, breath, over the tops of chimneys, the houses exhaling their blacks.

If he had learned French, like Charlotte, maybe he'd have had the chance to go abroad, on another railway line perhaps, to France or Sweden or Belgium.

He would have worked indoors or outdoors, if only the railroads would have taken him back.

They'd establish themselves at Thorp Green, Annii and Brannii, and then their father would come to visit them, come see his two children in their well-adjusted stations. How well they were all doing for themselves, his children.

They'd managed to enshrine themselves in a safe-to-say proud household.

Halls connected to halls.

Each night the table would be lavishly spread. All of the Robinsons, they'd lovingly eat together as one.

*

Some nights, late at night, their sister Anne believes she hears voices in the hallway. There is a light, a little boy's laugh, she imagines, that lights upon, lands within, her Gondal fantasies transposed to the great halls of Thorp Green. During the night, the voices change, as she herself flits in and out of dream, in and out of trying to listen, to really know, the source of the sounds in the hall. Edmund, William, the curate, drawing teacher, the Master, her once young pupil, her brother, all these men canvas the walls surrounding her in the flower of sexes.

She's not an artist. It's Branwell's job to give the boy drawing lessons, just as Mr. William Robinson of Leeds had done for Branwell.

Something descends here on this end of the house, as Anne tries to sleep it away in the quarters of her room. Emily is back in Haworth, Gondal, but she, Anne, must instruct. Those entrusted to her must not fall prey to the ways of the world. She's heard how they talk, out towards the barns. Some nights she imagines them wandering all over the great hall, the grounds, left to run free. She should get up now and go check to make sure everything's all right, that the girls are all in their beds.

She's to go walking through the hall, not taking her candle.

The shadows are afraid of the fire. What if one were to slip.

She trusts vision to moonlight through windows that open at the other end of the hall. Down below climb the lush shrubs, to the expanses of Thorp Green, the grounds of the Robinsons.

Boys need not only firmness, but also guiding hands, like the horse being broken in, trained, and reined.

Days there seemed no end to the life he could feel swelling

up inside him. To get somewhere in this life, you had to keep moving forward. There is no freedom for man without money.

That was the reality someone like Young Edmund might never be exposed to, made humble and vulnerable before. He could easily break this boy. What did their brother see there with his young charge. Young Edmund, one day you'll see, men, too, had their rituals to mate.

Perhaps he was already feeling this need inside him to reach out, the Young Master. Branwell wants to tell him it was all right to be curious, that there might be all sorts of flowers. But Branwell doesn't want to spoil Edmund.

Yes, it's through touching things that we come to know them.

He could tell him all about the men he'd met working on the railroad, down around there, the watermen. Some thought it was just hearsay. There were laborers who lived in packs in huts near the canal that ran nearby the station.

Young Edmund wants to know if these were Irishmen. He says it with the gasp of excitement. Were they like Branwell.

Had he ever told the boy about Angria. He should see the kings who lived there. They are tall, strongly built men. He should see the horses they ride, alongside the dogs that keep them in line.

He'll show the boy how to approach the landscape of his home differently.

It's as though there might be a wall built around this place.

It's like it's an enchanted land, Thorp Green, all for them.

He points out to him that cherry tree there, burst into a lace made up of white flowers.

But his parents don't really want him going around the stables, into the stables, not too much. They get scared, nervous. They can sense these things in you, the horses.

They'd walk a little further, a little closer to the stables, each day.

They were just going to draw, to sketch, to paint the roses, to try to focus on that. There were better roses, up around the stables, one of the gardeners comes by to tell them. Over that time, the roses began to grow much wilder.

Were boys after all hardy trees, able to resist every assault upon their morals. Should he and the boy try a match of fisticuffs. He had not grown much taller since he was fourteen.

Tell him, Young Edmund. Just tell him when you want to stop.

He'd have to work on this boy's imagination, when all he wanted to talk about was vipers.

Does he know the name of those birds up in that tree. They're redbreasts, also called thrushes. They read, chirp along, like you did today over your reading, with that pleasant little thrushing. Yes, the boy's pronunciation had been coming along quite nicely, all thanks to his instruction.

He deserves a trip to the stables just for that.

Only the adult male robins have that red there. Like Branwell, Young Edmund has noticed. Hand him his pencil. When he draws his namesake, the robin, he could shade it in like this. See.

He can show him some things if he doesn't tell his parents, in the stable. He could have a little drink there sometime. Just one. Just this once.

Branwell wants the boy to notice his own breast as broad, so he fills it up with fresh air straight from the boy's parents' land.

The boy has a face milder than any man he's yet come across.

Young Edmund, you must guard your splendors.

Caprice, Young Edmund, could be a man's downfall.

He wants to bring apples for the horses next time.

The boy's mother is interested in what Branwell might do all alone at night in Monk's House, when not tending to her son. He says he'll write her a poem or two, just to show her. He's happened to mention he writes poetry, hasn't he.

She could help Branwell with his poetry, as she knew some of the right people you needed to know.

Really.

Yes.

Yesterday she showed Branwell the picture she'd once tried to paint of herself, to ask her son's tutor his honest, professional opinion. Young Edmund had begun to sulk a bit from the lack of attention, to stick out his tongue from the corner of Monk's House.

Now, Young Edmund, a poet needs not only leisure but money to pursue his vocation. He's perhaps heard of the poet Hartley Coleridge. No. Well, then they'd read him tomorrow. Branwell keeps with him Hartley's translation of one of the Odes. His father had left him enough money to make literature his life's pursuit. It was to be concentrated upon with great singularity. A man, like Northangerland, on the other hand, must go this road alone. And it does take a certain dedication that the wealthier of us . . . Branwell cleared his throat. The rest of us had to teach little boys like you, Edmund.

Oh, yes, he gets some joy out of it.

But not as much joy as he would if everyone knew who he was.

He means men of some real substance. There were men that one called men of the world. One day Edmund would understand. He knows he doesn't have any money right now, but just wait. One day he would be flush.

You see, he wanted to be one of them. Well, he was one. He just didn't have the money; and he wanted to be recognized as one of them. That's all, that little difference between him and you.

*

There were anatomy lessons to be found in poetry. One just had to know where to look. There was his line of the smell of sweet melancholy. Here. He'd show him and his mother a bit of what he means. The body and the soul were the same thing, one could see it in a rose. There were no words for it, this paradise of the soul you could experience by just trying to open yourself, like a flower, a rose. You could never tell the secret.

His teacher points the inside of the rose out to the boy. What did Young Edmund think of that. Affection and feelings, did it embarrass them. Watch as he made it open up even further, how it shined inside a bit still wet, from the last rain. He takes one wet yellow rose from a vase he's placed on the windowsill.

Now be careful your finger doesn't catch the thorn, or you will bleed like the petals in his hand now are.

Just like they have to watch out for nails in the barn.

Branwell has been promising to take him there, again.

Now why was he blushing.

Couldn't he control himself.

The lack of words, no more need for words, that was nature's harmony.

He holds the petals in his hand, makes a tight fist over them.

*

The family takes summer by the sea, in the rented Cliff properties at Scarborough. They have the finest views there. The son is always listed on the visitors list as Master Robinson. It was where Anne wanted to be buried, when she died.

There are thirteen suites of rooms in the house they rent. It's three stories, a smart watering place. From behind the house they'd set off, Branwell and his pupil, for the museum one reached by following a path down under a bridge. Have the Robinsons heard of Darwin. Or is it too early yet for that. Branwell was trying to spark a continued interest in the young lad. The museum at Scarborough held fossils, geological specimens. These stones could be dated and prove to any and all the starting point of the Bible holds no real basis.

If he can just get close enough to the boy's mother, Branwell's position in this world might become more assured, and he might rise above the post of mere tutor. He believes this though Branwell can tell he hasn't completely won over her husband. The wife accompanies Young Edmund and the tutor on some of the walks they take, where it is Branwell's job to point out things that might be of interest to them.

Towards the end of summer they would return back to the house at Thorp Green, and Anne would think nothing of the way she'd seen her brother and Mrs. Robinson holding the young boy's hand between the two of them, no differently than she herself held the hands of her own pupils, and would continue to until it was too late, and they no longer needed her, soon to be married, wives. That's what the sisters are to grow up to be. That's what their mother has in mind for them all.

*

Around each other, between the two of them, her brother and the boy appear to incite unspeakable, transferable fevers, a poetry that's flooding their movement, firing their racing around the grounds.

Young Edmund seems to respond to Northangerland.

They are bundles of warmth, alight in the sun. He has the boy sit there, sketch. Branwell is there, going off to see about the stables, the horses, the grooms.

Branwell had made friends with all the servants. Now he had some friends to go shoot pheasants with. He'd laughed gleefully along with them, sharing in their jokes.

Anne won't know how off in Brussels Charlotte had begun to fall in love, with her Master, her professor, tracing her affections like something from a story she and Branwell created for themselves to pass the time.

Anne knows how Branwell drinks with the hired help. He himself is hired help. He takes pleasure at Thorp Green secretly, his fear only adding to the nature of it, that it might be discovered. Everyone might now know. But where was the future in forever having to turn away from what you felt you wanted, what you felt you wanted to feel.

What could he do to make one keep reading.

Now was the time to make something happen.

Dear Reader, you want to be told now that you've understood. That he might be doing just what you think he might be, and in just what way. You want to be sure.

The grooms show him a number of ways to untie those animals they keep leashed up.

That's the way it works.

This constant daydreaming was irresponsible.

Northangerland was the one who might bring a different light most assuredly to everything. He was Northangerland. That's what he wanted Young Edmund to call him from now on.

Anne kept her eyes on him when she could.

Young Edmund's mother must mark the way her son's face lights up the moment his tutor enters the room to collect his charge. Anne doesn't know if she is dreaming or not, if her brother really holds onto the boy like that. In the hall, the bushes outside made shadows all along the wall. Perhaps what made those shadows there was only the holly bush between the window and porch.

The wind moved limbs like hands, hands rearranging, impressions on the walls.

A shade was made, a sort of nun-like veil, all over the walls, and that stretched down towards the carpet. Anne could never have dreamed the things she'd stumble out of her room, to believe she might find, some night, early morning, had she not actually seen them. How could she.

Is that what she wants. Is that what she wants to see. Was it Edmund. The small thing held in larger hands. Or was it one of the girls.

She couldn't help but notice that the frame of the young boy Edmund had begun to fill out somewhat.

In the morning, Young Edmund dashes out of the house, runs down to Monk's House calling Brannii. Anne has heard him using that very name, their secret name. What had her brother been filling this boy's mind with.

What would her brother be doing there in the house, that late at night, if that was him she saw. He must walk up from Monk's House each night. Up to the main house, up to the manor.

Or one of the grooms who has lost his way slips out of one of the other rooms.

It's a large house, especially for the hired help. Like her, like her brother.

She heard something. Who was outside, there on the landing. Anne would have to go see, her heart beating in her ears.

The shadows of trees thrown over the walls painted in a picture, of limbs, and arms, around a body; a boy, in shadows, only waiting to be uncovered, gain with the wind a bit more stature, to rise up beside what appears to be another body. Two bodies were surely out there together. One of them is not quite as tall as the other.

Limbs only cradle other limbs.

Her cheeks warm and burn brightly as she lowers herself down towards the other end of the hall, as the shadows move along over the walls, glad she hasn't brought a candle. She's imagined she's seen enough, in the laboring shadows. She tries to put them together. She tries to be quiet on the threshold of the door to her bedroom, tries to return to bed quietly.

Tries to drown her mind out by closing her eyes.

She'd not seen one of them kissing the other on the lips.
Outside, in the night, the mating call of frogs.
They are descending on Spring.
They lurch their voices out, so others of their kind may be attracted, the darkness, drawn, something they'd risk.
They might be found.
Her brother, outside, as pale as the moon, is wandering around the grounds. It must be him, out for a walk, coming up through the shrubbery this late at night. There's a male wandering around the Robinsons' grounds. She looks out from a window, out to where they'd surely catch their death of cold.
She's dreamed the carpet in the hall under her feet damp weeds, brushwood, the wall hangings scant foliage. She could never simply imagine such things. She dreamed it.
While she's there, at Thorp Green, Anne will feel she's gotten her fill of mankind and his disgusting ways.

*

Young Edmund wants to play at being a peasant at court, but the grooms all recognize him as Master. Young Edmund has surprised them all one night in the stables, one night when Branwell, too, is there.
What's he doing.
Out of the house, at this hour.
Let him stay.
Not if they value their jobs.
They can't be sure he wouldn't talk in the morning. There were some things that shouldn't be getting up to the Hall.

Flowers of different stripes lay all around out there, scattered around the stables by the breezes, Irish roses. They rest up against the hard stones, the softness of their flesh, their green stems, now just forms in the dark.

He'd have to be carefully guided up the flags.

He's made a mess of his clothes, being there in the stables like that.

He speaks to the boy as if the boy were there, always there, still. Youth, Health, Hope, he had them at hand. These were all things the boy had before him. Why do leaves feel the way they do under our skin, if we aren't to catch ourselves touching them, moving them back, pulling at them now, to strip our switch.

It would only be natural, walking like that, for him to take his hand. See how soft it felt. The inside of the jacket, like rabbit skin, pheasant feathers, wool, warm down.

Branwell rambles.

Yes, the boy would have to learn to identify the way connections were made. We were made to fit to things, through the right words, our lots.

His form was so tender still.

It must be guided right up into manhood.

This was Branwell's job, what he was there for, what he'd been hired to do.

He was there to take care of him.

*

The boy had taken to him. A year after he's been there, Branwell is still said to be wonderfully valued. For months at a time, all they'd hear, all anyone would hear from Thorp Green, was nothing but good. Anne's never liked it much, but Branwell seems to have really found a place for himself.

Out there in Monk's House, he's begun his solitary Secret

Play, in which he's writing the type of character he wants to become. He's doing it alone. He could be anyone he'd like to be in the writing.

You could not believe the way the Robinsons treated the hired help. His favorite face-card the Jack, Branwell played cards with the grooms in the stables. The Jack occupies a peculiar position in the deck. Yes, he's royalty. But he's married to no one.

What's a vestal virgin, one of them asks, anticipating the coming punchline.

Almost a redundancy.

Make a fist.

Come here, they'll show him how, how to do it even better, strike more assuredly home.

Were there any differences between playing at boxing, wrestling, and performing the slithering more in earnest.

How fast did one get up, brush himself off, after they'd pinned you.

You've got to be quick, dunk.

It is called practice.

Now what was the difference between a man's tongue and a horse's.

They'll let him feel the difference. Here, feel that.

He tells them his pupil's been wanting to see the horses again.

Around the stables, Young Edmund could be a delightful fellow, asking if the grooms were not his servants, if didn't they have to do what he told them to do. He liked the horses.

Does a foal feel more happy as a foal.

That little feeling in his head like a thorn in his flesh, that was only the worrying of a coming punishment that kept creeping in. One had to learn to keep it at bay, if one wanted to go further, if one ever wanted to have one's own story. Did he really want to grow up to be like his father.

Their brother had been seen in the house, when he wasn't supposed to be.

What was he doing there.

What was he doing so near, so close to the bedroom of the Mistress of the house. Her closed door was guarded and locked now.

He may have been only looking for Edmund.

But wasn't Edmund to take his lessons with him in Monk's House.

Mr. Robinson has been keeping a watch out now, down around the stables.

He almost never used to go down around there.

The horses would be brought up to Mr. Robinson, when he needed one for some business or other.

They were considering a problem, a problem for them all, their futures.

It was the path their brother had now begun to set himself down upon, once again.

Branwell would come into the house, late at night, to borrow some books. He'd gone through everything he had out there with him in Monk's House. They had the Odyssey, Paradise Lost, Sophocles, Euripides, all inside.

He was going to succumb to temptation.

Finally, what was going to become of this aberrant brother.

A boy's legs dashed up stairs, troubled pleasure soon chastised by fear.

What had their brother been teaching him.

That was no way for him to conduct himself in a house. He knows what his parents would say. These people had been good to him. Had their brother ever been this well off, at any other time in his entire life. Was it not her word, Anne's good word, that had brought him here. Was he not settled.

She was concerned about Branwell and his conduct at Thorp Green. The boy was going wild, anyone could see it, if they'd just take the time to look. They could hear the way he talks, the words that had come from his very young mouth. His parents couldn't be too busy with themselves for him.

A mind must make something of the evidence that's been put before it. Anne believes she knows what's going on. She believes she knows everything. There must be more to this story. All their brother's stories, his childhood stories, they had continued, those facts and fabrications of his, with no way now to distinguish behind them the real promise Branwell had once displayed. He must believe he's still living in one of his poems, there at Thorp Green.

He was trying to train poetry into the Robinsons' son.

Someone had to take things in hand, before they went too far.

He'd told him that this line, this line there in his wrist, when he cuffed his fingers around it, like that, was the heart, beating faster.

He took the boy by the hand when they went for their walk, told him all about Maria. Out in Monk's House, he's heard her, he says, but could it just be the boy's voice, or the grooms' voices. The wind playing at being her.

When there was no fire in the grate, you must learn to make your own.

129

One day this would all be Edmund's, all of this property. It would be. The boy asks Branwell if Maria was anything like his mother. A boy had to learn how to keep himself, Young Edmund. The boy had to see his mother wasn't always going to be there for him.

Was he going to be able to take it, all the world would one day require him to hold himself up against, move out against.

Now Branwell has made him cry.

He is talking to him, talking to him still in his head, when the boy isn't there with him anymore at the end of the day in Monk's House.

There was the glass in the window he could walk up to and see his face in now, the massive forehead, well-set eyes, a fine, intellectual expression, the nose a strong nose.

Is that how they all saw him.

The thick lips indicated a self-indulgence, and coarse lines were beginning to appear around his mouth. It would be only more pronounced, out in the sun. He feels the need to blot himself out. But he wasn't going to drink tonight, he had promised himself that.

*

He'd come home for the Christmas holiday with Anne, and he'd seemed to be in better spirits than the last time he'd been home. Over the summer, they'd all noticed, he'd seemed so preoccupied. His moods swung wildly, in a way they hoped he was better able to control out at Thorp Green.

But he seems anxious to be away from Thorp Green for too long.

Charlotte is glad he's so wondrously valued in his situation there, though she's a bit troubled he no longer seems to be able to enjoy his time at home with them.

A word he mumbles over dinner sounds like treachery.

Something must be bringing on these incessant attacks of illness. Home again for a short holiday in June, he had been so irritable. He's not drinking again, is he. His sisters were afraid to ask him. Might their father suspect something.

He has to get back to Thorp Green, as if there were some unfinished business.

In October, back home for a brief spell, he'd still seemed ill, to Charlotte especially.

Then he and Anne had returned for Christmas. Immediately he'd slunk off from their sight, off into his own room, to work on a poem he claims to be writing. He's still writing poetry, then, though she doesn't seem to know who he is anymore. She never sees him.

There was a peculiarity now that had grown up inside him, that he might try to let bloom further, like a Romantic, if he were only far enough away from home, if he watered it enough alone, as when, in Monk's House, he was able to write with no one watching over his shoulder.

He and Anne would return to Thorp Green in January.

But Anne must save herself.

The next time they come home in June, Anne would announce for once and for all she is not going back. Their brother could return without her. He would just have to.

There were some things going on there of which she'd never be able to approve.

Anne would miss her charges, the girls, but still, they would all be marrying soon, leaving home anyway. There would be no use for Anne then. She could only hope she'd taught them something they might carry with them for the rest of their days.

Anne leaves no clear record of what she actually saw, what she thought, what she believes happens at Thorp Green.

For two and a half years their brother had been there.

His eventual dismissal would be abrupt, as if something had been finally discovered, as if the man of the house suddenly had seen he didn't know how to watch out for his family. Whatever had been going on, it would have been going on the whole time Branwell had been there. It must have been.

A young boy's life had been placed in his hands.

When Branwell returns home, he'll have to be able to tell his family a good story why. It'll have to be persuasive enough. He'll have to be able to talk them into it, live as if he's living the end of a great love story.

*

That summer Branwell had announced he needed to get back earlier, sooner, to Thorp Green. He and Anne usually returned to Haworth to see their family before returning to go with the Robinson family to Scarborough.

He would never be able to go with them to Scarborough again.

He's forbidden.

He's no longer to care for Young Edmund.

One of the grooms could always bring Young Edmund up to Scarborough later. He didn't have to go with his parents. He could ride up alongside him all the way there. He could

go up later. He had been going for quite some time now
on the horses. He was old enough to be riding now, though
his father still didn't want him playing down around the
stables.

One of the grooms was to bring a horse up to him, the
gentlest one.

Young Edmund could use his new whip.

They'd have to give it some thought, leaving the boy all alone
with his tutor for a week or so, before joining them all at
Scarborough. They'd have to believe the boy would be fine
being left with Branwell, in his care.

All the other servants would still be around.

They'd have a whole week alone, no parents to bother
them. A vacation. No lessons. They could do anything,
anything Young Edmund would like to do. His parents could
be told a different story. They would be able to take their
meals alone, away from parents and sisters, while they enjoyed
the holiday.

There isn't a word for it yet, that he knows, his feelings.

Edmund's father had given him some money for ferrets.

His father had bought him a whip for a horse, but he's
not to be using it on the horse, not like that.

Here, Branwell would show him.

Does Young Edmund really believe he's big enough to
ride a horse, his own, all the way up to Scarborough.

That summer he wouldn't have to ride up there in the
coach with his family.

Now Edmund was to learn some independence.

He was to make his own decisions.

He was old enough.

There's a new railway line opening nearby Thorp Green.

While Edmund's family is away in Scarborough, they could go see it.

Young Edmund wants to know if Branwell had ever driven the train.

That day there would be speeches and celebrations, the festival, as if just for them. How far afield the Master would have the boy then from his mother.

Imagine he's wearing a muzzle.

The boy's parents would have to try and figure out why he's no longer speaking to them, once he gets to Scarborough.

There's no way he could ever tell them all Branwell had let him do when they were left alone.

In Scarborough, they would have all been expecting the boy much sooner than his arrival would actually be able to be recorded. All the guests for the season were duly noted in all the newspapers, papers where Branwell was still trying to publish every now and then an occasional poem.

In Scarborough, look at the way their son had acted then, traipsing about the beaches.

Who was he getting this from.

He'd become somewhat the expert in melodrama, hadn't he.

He was no longer anything like a son of theirs.

Only one person could be encouraging such things, to the point that his parents no longer recognized him. It was as if their son now believed there might be more important things than just his mother and his father. Was it not enough that their eldest daughter, one of Anne's charges, elopes with an actor. They'll have to find someone to take better care of him.

The day after the newspapers report Edmund to arrive in Scarborough, Branwell tells his family back home he's received his letter of dismissal.

Mr. Robinson would kill Branwell for having done this thing to his son.

He'd told Edmund he'd be back, back to see to him once he and his parents had returned from their summer away in Scarborough. If for some reason he wasn't, if for some reason he didn't, if there was anything more he needed to tell him, anything, he could write him, later.

Or Branwell could follow them up to Scarborough discreetly.

They could meet secretly once he was there.

Their gardener would be coming up to Scarborough, to help with the horses, all the baggage, as their normal groom could use an extra hand. Of course Branwell was no gardener. He's to be confused with no mere servant.

But in the wake of the coming scandal, not only would Branwell not return, but the aforementioned gardener would also disappear, shortly after that summer.

Who else had been seen, where they shouldn't have been, and how.

Young Edmund's parents would have to try to bring his character back into line somehow now. The boy must be made to take up with more appropriate hobbies than spending his time around the stables on the outer reaches of his parents' property.

Their son would have to be sent away.

It was the only way.

They'll consign him to a clergyman. They're going to.

When they get him home, the family physician will have to inspect him. They have to be sure. A boy his age can't be blamed, but they want to make sure he hasn't been permanently damaged. He was only a boy. He could have been damaged. In the future they want their son kept as far away from Yorkshire as possible, until he's completely matured.

The Reverend they're sending him to will instruct him on how to behave properly in later life. He'll be staying with this Reverend for a number of years, four or five, until he's eighteen. The Reverend must be able to write Mr. and Mrs. Robinson how Young Edmund passes his time with him in complete purity and innocence.

Edmund was only a simple boy.

*

Around the environs of Haworth they'll claim Branwell has fathered a child illegitimately. They'll claim they've seen it in a letter. They copied down the letter they saw. That's final proof. Charlotte wouldn't be able to believe such a thing; but such sayings were the material of legends, kept alive in some families.

A son or daughter will believe they descend from one of the Brontës. They hold onto these things they pass down.

Some would say he'd fathered a child, but the child had died, like in a poem he'd written.

A love until death, he tells Emily how he might have had that.

It's Emily that's close to him when he returns home to Haworth. Not Anne, who might have seen something in the hall, in the environs of Thorp Green. She'll never speak of it. Even the male servants had to be good for something. They had to learn to keep things to themselves.

*

There's a letter quoted that will never be seen. A few facts were always open to another interpretation. Branwell will tell them what it says, all of its black contents, how and why the Robinsons want to get rid of him, want to get him away from Edmund. They must trust him. From the swells and hollow of the mossy turf, the shade of the trees, he is returning. Branwell is returning for good this time. Emily will be happy to have their brother home again.

He stands in the road in front of the parsonage, with paper in his fisted hand. He must tell them all what it says. Give them a version they could continue to try to live with, to base life under the same roof upon.

If he were to suffer, his years might seem in some way justified, if there had been this love, this life that had been lost. Without such a heart broken, he'd have no story. He'd be nothing but a boy of twenty-eight, underdeveloped in all ways, the best years of his life wasted. He's too near pleasure for repentance he believes, and too near death for hope.

His heart feels just a shard now.

Had he spared a thought for anyone but himself.

Had he.

The birches swim over his head, a sickly peevishness now palling him.

What did the letter say. He's received a letter. Read the letter to them, Branwell. What news did the Robinsons send from Scarborough.

He's tired.

He'll share the news with them later.

They can't expect Branwell to play writing games with them now, not anymore, to run with them all outside over the moors, not now.

He must be left undisturbed all this evening.

Not one sound yet from his room all evening, Emily sounds concerned.

The tea has been laid out, but when he comes downstairs, he then begins to cry.

Branwell, what was the matter.

Anne, bring him some tea. He takes a seat on their red horsehair sofa.

He's been accused of something. They'll never believe it.

The sudden, early, obscure closure of what might have been his noble career.

*

The men he kept company with down at the Black Bull weren't to come to the parsonage, but he'll go to them. He'll try to bury himself there once more. Though this time the offense, the dismissal, is much graver. He'll have to be prepared with a story for everyone.

His home was not his. It no longer felt that way. Not with their sister Charlotte back there, always following him with her eyes, believing she knows everything, that he is truly nothing.

Troubled pleasure soon chastened by fear. That's what he'd had.

He could go with Emily to take her dog out.

They'd lost him past all recall, whether they knew it yet or not.

He doesn't know what one means by the grace of manhood. Wind shivers between the branches of the ash. He doesn't know how to contain all he doesn't know what to do with. Maybe he had needed to play with other boys, to learn how to be one better.

He dreamed these nights, of another boy he'd once walked the moors with, as he now walks with Emily. Through the village, back to meadows, the fields, where in all the excitement of then being so strong, so alive, they would fall down rolling towards the ground and over each other. Just to see who was the most.

Even as a boy he'd worn these glasses he was never to take off, sometimes knocked off in fighting. If he'd come home without them, if he'd lost them, their father would want to know exactly what had happened, where he'd been, and with whom, what he'd been doing.

There were times when he'd just rather not have gone back home. He was going to have to get his story set, about what had happened between him and the boy he'd been off with. They'd been playing, fighting. They weren't really, walking down roads and back, up before respective homes.

In dreams, he was guilty of nothing. Only once he'd woken, facing his family. Things would have to be lied about.

He'd not been afraid then in the slightest.

Deep down in their woods, the two of them had been all out of breath together. Walking shouldered up against the wind they were not to have gone off like that. They played a game where they took turns being the deer. Or they imagined they were those very horses, let out of their stables. They pawed foaming up at each other, like those, in their excitement, like them on hind-legs raised up.

Until falling back on all fours.

Wild dogs followed them home, barking at their heels, as if they'd been caught, brought back into line.

He's lying again.

He'd wake up to try and check, make sure his breathing was still even, pull back the blanket, to stare at the body thoroughly covered. Even in sleep, he'll have to check up on himself. But he can see he hasn't just been dreaming, with the way the sheets are marked.

He fumbled too often, a skittish stuttering, starting as his mind split off down along different tracks simultaneously. He's not confident yet in his fiction. He hasn't yet learned how to rein himself in.

Maybe eventually they'd do a larger canvas.

In this world, he could only be a genius if he showed the marks of one early. The first Mr. Robinson had assured him of the truth of this.

They begin to exist in their own private sanctity, these boys kept close to their masters.

Between lessons of Latin and drudgery, they'd been wrestling, pawing each other.

Crying out would have to be learned to be controlled.

That's how they carried on in the stables, where they didn't know any better.

Stories cover other stories up. He knows how to put a good face on it all.

Such lessons are done with by supper.

At the table, he'd be more silent, want to go up to his

room, want to be left alone. He can't wait for tomorrow, when he can go out again.

Mr. Robinson claims to know exactly what their brother has been up to. And he's to stay away from his family, since what he's been doing was bad beyond expression. Branwell would say he's been told never to return again to Thorp Green. It's in Mr. Robinson's letter, he says. They wouldn't believe the things he's said about Branwell. Clearly Mr. Robinson wouldn't deign to write such things plainly. But Branwell will tell them what it says, what it all means.

What if their father were to know what his son's been doing.

This letter his family never sees.

He has been discovered. They know now who Branwell really is. And if he didn't want everyone to know, he was to break off now and forever any and all communications with Mr. Robinson's family. Mr. Robinson would tolerate no further attempts. He's threatened to shoot Branwell, if he ever catches him around the estate of Thorp Green again.

Branwell says he burned the letter as soon as he got it. But he know its contents by heart.

*

The realm of fantasy must be left now. They must accept their fates. They will have to work. Emily was not to marry. Nor Anne. Nor their brother. Only Charlotte, who would one day be in the position, when they were all gone, to speak for them all. To say what her sisters sought, in their work, what her sisters were looking to find, to create.

Their early stories could be changed, in order to make

them seem more realistic, to move them more towards an audience, to be more rooted in families that others could fathom, relate to, not just those who knew Angria or Gondal.

This was not the first time their brother had returned home in disgrace, but this time Branwell has gone too far, Charlotte thinks. He's lost to them, she says.

How would he ever convince his sisters it wouldn't happen again, that he could ever improve. Nobody would give him another chance now. He'd have to live with this, for as long as he lived.

She believes he doesn't want to get better.

In the morning, he just wants to go back to sleep. Their father, moving around the house, tries to rouse him. And his sisters. Branwell remembers where he is. Haworth. Where the graves are all right outside the window.

Because they will never let him forget, he'll never be able to, how he's been brought back, here, this low.

He has his story all ready for them all.

Did he know exactly what he'd done wrong.

The boy hadn't turned on him, had he.

Anne had seen him, once or twice, where he wasn't supposed to be.

Had Young Edmund said something.

He'd never punished him. He'd been so gentle with the boy.

Anne had watched her brother become a different person in that house.

He had to learn how to control himself, how to keep a firmer hand on himself, from now on. To keep working on himself. Keep working.

His thoughts had to be made pure again.

He had to learn how to put behind him how he'd lived there with the boy, how they'd drawn their horses together.

They'd gone for walks, down to the stream where they'd bent to drink. He'd taught him the Latin names for things.

He's never to get that close to the house at Thorp Green again. The closest he would get would be to the houses of friends nearby, after he'd been out drinking all hours of the morning, after wandering the moors.

He's said to be keeping up a correspondence with someone in the area of Thorp Green. Though those letters are not seen, either. Branwell will tell them down at the bar what they've all said.

He deserved this hurt. Their brother should feel this hurt. Charlotte points that out to Emily. He moves around the house like he knows what he's done, like the dog that knows he's disappointed his master, but stealthily attempting to get back close to the hand that feeds, judge how kind it might become again, approaching from the same corner he'd slink back to.

He slumped his shoulders under some pressure they couldn't see.

He slouched up from the sleep he tried to maintain all day, to avoid the lights in the parsonage, outside on the moors, slipping down along shadows falling on the walls, trying to avoid their father's voice.

Like a shadow now slipping across their father's eye.

They blinked, and he'd come clearer, or he's already disappeared from the room.

Their father's sight was getting worse.

He needed Charlotte there. They'd no longer be fine

without her. She had returned home, from Brussels, to find her brother like Anne, there for good now.

The news had had to be broken to Charlotte gently.

There was nothing else in Brussels for her, where she no longer felt wanted sufficiently. M. Heger certainly did not need her.

*

No longer any love of boyhood, as Branwell's not of his right mind some nights. He wasn't who he was supposed to be. He awoke to find himself alone in a bed in the parsonage in their father's house. Stunning, drowning his mind, distressed, that's how Charlotte refers to their brother Branwell in this ill state, the fault of his own making.

He'd refer to his illness repeatedly in the letters he writes. He'd fallen in love with the wife of his master's house, and she'd fallen in love with him. She was seventeen years older than him, but he swears that feeling was pure and true. He writes himself shattered in body and broken in mind.

Their father spoke of beings with depraved appetites, beings with sickly imaginations, beings who had learned to embrace the art of self-torment, diligently, zealously employing themselves in the creation of a world wholly imaginary, a world one could never actually have had a real life in. It was of their own making. One could never live like that.

It was because of all of those dreams the world one must still walk through became gloomy and insupportable.

Just like his God, who'd turned his back on this world. If he'd ever been there in the first place.

They would have sad work with him now.

He was not going to talk. He was not going to tell them. He remains too drunk to talk. He was not going to tell Charlotte.

The wife, he told everyone else, had wanted to be his, to marry their brother, had wanted him to stay with her at Thorp Green. As soon as her husband died, he told everyone, she would send for him. Their ages did not matter. And she'd wanted to give him her money. They were going to be together. She was going to give him the land of Thorp Green.

He writes to friends for money, for drinks. He tells his sisters the money comes from Mrs. Robinson.

This woman has tempted him, their only brother, their father's only son, led him astray.

Anne had had the presence of mind to leave before it was too late.

Anne had seen how she'd raised her daughters, to look only for husbands, and even their unnatural interest in the stable hands.

Anne sits quietly. She doesn't work for them anymore.

How long would she be able to keep this quiet, how long, the shame. It gnaws at their consciences, alone in their rooms. It had crept into the house now, up to the windows. It had gotten in. Lived in the corners where their brother sat, blushed cheeks all shades of red.

The fire, the draft, hotness she feels howling along inside, trying to trap her. This was bound to be the death of them all, he was.

*

He'd set himself on a course. He begins to suffer from a chronic bronchitis, a cough that won't go away. It could drive him to become more violent, like one of his characters. He wants to

145

see just how far he could take himself into the cold debauchery of the bars like the Black Bull he'd once tried to leave behind. He decides to embrace them warmly, hold them passionately, as no better prospects are left. Now more than ever, rather than himself, he wants to become his character Northangerland.

Their father couldn't quiet him, though he'd try, with prayers, more prayers, his thoughts of the scripture, all the hopes and dreams he'd once had for his beautiful son. Their father could no longer bear to look at him, his son that had gone from him, had slipped so far into these fits of longing.

Their father had never even called out for his own wife like that, the way Branwell now called out for her, Maria, Mrs. Robinson, Lydia, called through an endless litany of names that went through the house in the middle of the night, out from his room.

He was the first of all of their father's children to publish a poem. He'd publish six, before any of his sisters, in two newspapers. And he'd go on to publish fifteen, sixteen, seventeen poems, in three, four newspapers. The Halifax Guardian, the Bradford Herald, the Leeds Intelligencer. He'd written all these poems at Luddenden Foot. He just had to copy them out again. In one he'll call the first Afghan War Winter's War, a piece he'd written around the British retreat from Kabul in 1842, about how men died inside in the chilly silence, about how their stories would stop there, twenty thousand–odd troops and camp followers dead.

Newspaper publications are even better than when he was a boy, and for his sisters had produced the two volumes he'd written as Young Soult, the Rhymer. He could rewrite Percy's last sonnet, a sonnet on peaceful death, painful life, the lone shore, eternal, earth, heaven. He'll publish it in the Bradford

Herald, and in the Halifax Guardian, in two separate newspapers. The Robinsons of Thorp Green read such.

He'll publish poems in the newspapers under the name of Northangerland. That way he believes he can say whatever he wants, and nobody will know who he is anymore. He is Northangerland. Northangerland was a man who had never had to conduct himself appropriately.

His shame stretched before him, along the wilds of a lonely Haworth, where he'd walked once with Maria, hadn't he. When just a boy. She'd held him, held expecting nothing.

His emotions crossed each other, doubled back, to himself in again, to wreck him.

Night approached, lowering clouds to lie upon the ground. Haworth was where he'd become who he'd always be, nothing more.

Look at his sisters, looking at him like they were scared of him.

But he could not write without the prop of his hero, Northangerland.

His sisters try to tame contrary emotions around him, to get him down safely into the pages that would become their books, each in her own way filling in the gaps in her knowledge with her imagination. Their portraits distort, as they wrestle with the sides of Branwell's increasingly jagged existence, the collapsing personality.

Just seeing how it had swallowed him, he'd made Angria so much easier for Charlotte to leave for good. He was the one who couldn't grow up from it.

He had a certain daring, according to Emily.

To Anne, he's a warning.

*

A world of eternal sleep, that's what he wants.

His friend John Brown has proposed a trip to Liverpool, John Brown the village sexton and gravedigger. He was someone Branwell could confide in.

Branwell must get better, for his family's sake.

They had to try to pull him from the drinking spell he seemed intent on never emerging from. There's gossip all through Haworth. The black sheep of the flock, the Parson's very own son. Nothing but the braying of asses, all around him, Branwell notices. It would be better for everyone involved if the people of Haworth did not see him like this.

In case he hadn't noticed there was someone he was supposed to be.

A trip to Wales with his good friend John Brown might be just the thing, they all agreed, his sisters and their father. There with him, with John Brown in Liverpool, in Wales, he could see the sweet scenery of the sea.

Surely he feels himself going blind with sadness.

And the drinking was only making him sadder.

And John Brown was a man who knew how to take other men by the heel. He could tell John Brown, tell him what's on his mind. John Brown was Worshipful Grand Master of the Lodge of the Three Graces. Let the two men have a little heart to heart.

There were parts of those letters, John knew, he was to black out, ones he'd been getting from Branwell from his posts.

This latest escapade had the sound of one of those adulterous stories he and his sisters had raised themselves on since childhood. How had John felt, receiving that lock of hair, a strand Branwell had told him was Mrs. Robinson's. Lydia. He'd wanted John to have it, a piece of her. Did he still have it. What had he done with it.

He'd not signed his name to that letter, because while he was away he had truly become someone else, and he wanted John to know.

He'd been writing about an imaginary Lydia for John before he'd even gone off to his post at Thorp Green. His imagination now could fall back on that, all he'd trained himself to imagine all along. He was to be loved this way. He was to be loved back. He wanted to give John a feeling of something carnal.

The golden halo of fiction needs to surround these close talks of theirs.

Branwell needs John Brown to believe he'd offered up not only his youth to this woman, with her position and all her money, but all his talents. Everyone he tells her husband is dying, and how he'd seen him treating her horribly.

His sister Anne believes such a place riddles one's soul through with vice. Mrs. Robinson, Anne says, was not beautiful but depraved, an awful woman.

Lydia has been forbidden to have any contact with Branwell, Branwell says, or she'll lose all her money, her home, her property, everything. He hears from those around those parts that she's made herself sick with her love for him, she is dying of love.

He'd been sent to Liverpool, then to tour North Wales, to try to recover from the dismissal. His sister Emily says he's hopeless, but she says such things in understanding and love. From North Wales, he writes to Charlotte. He promises to try to do better. But she expects little will come from such promises.

Perhaps, in the future, he might work with John Brown. That might keep him happy. Branwell could be John's secretary, help him keep track of gravestones that have been ordered. Maybe even help him fashion some one day. How would Branwell like that.

There may be no peace, while he is still in the house with them.

*

He finds himself on the floor, as hard as stone, hard as his breast must be now to the outside world. He rubs his lips up against the skin of the pillow, deep in one of his nightmares, dragging himself back up onto the bed, smashing against the wood underneath it, trying to say something that won't come out in the right way.

A voice in the house coming from the hall calls him out onto the landing, a voice as sweet and as young, as yet unchanged, as his mother's, Maria's, a young boy's. He can't sort out this that all takes place in a dream now, once back home from his trip with John.

Maria, it was Maria who'd called to him, kept calling to him, called him out into the hall. She'd come back, the one who'd flashed up in the young boy's face. He had to grasp her in the hall.

That's where he's run into Emily, Emily bringing him a candle up to his room.

Emily looks a vision in this light.

He shouldn't just lie alone in bed all day in the dark, red bed curtains pulled.

He's writing a letter to John. He'd gone to see if there was anyone in the hall. He'd thought he'd heard someone out there. Just Emily making her rounds through the house, lighting up the candles. He thought he heard someone out in the graveyard, calling to him.

John might be out there, waiting for him.

John would forgive him anything no matter what he's done.

The opium helps him feel his own suffering. It courses through him in dreams the opium helps bring, dreams that turn the tender look of Emily's face a bit softer, like Edmund's, a bit more towards the motherly, like the skin of a peach. She saw the way he was with William. They all saw the way he was with William.

He's talking alone to himself in his room again tonight, his candle burned down by now, as one after another of his sisters makes her way through the hall outside his room. He knows their steps. Charlotte believes she can hear him laughing.

His eyesight dimmed to the slightest pinhole, their father seldom moves himself these days.

John Brown bends down over a grave, to chisel in a name, while men around him gather, outside in the graveyard. He sees them. He knows they are out there.

The trees, they lean in the breeze. They grow the way the wind blows them.

Emily must see to Branwell, if anyone will. Charlotte has her own things to think about, her own hands full already. She doesn't understand why her Master, M. Heger, has not answered two of her letters. Perhaps his wife has seen them. Perhaps she has taken them away and hidden them.

In Brussels, the buildings slept behind white gates, nestled up close together. The doors latched securely.

They held lessons in the garden, in Brussels.

She had been one of the fresh-faced girls.

It was a veritable Paradise, a long protected building, like a castle. The trees swept gently near it, though never touching, never laying an errant branch too close to a window.

She'd slept there dreaming of the Duke of Wellington. The Duke wore shiny black boots up almost to his knees. He carried his sword. And a wooden club. Around his waist was a great belt, made of gold brocade. He wore a high, white shirt, under the great black coat that was trimmed in fur in places, just like Master Heger's.

All French now reminds Charlotte of her Master, in Brussels, where she won't be able to return. Such luxury will not be permitted her.

No one has answered any of her letters. She had wanted to believe only that he had not wanted to see her go, even if he wanted nothing more from her than her friendship.

If their brother was not going to make something of himself, if he was just going to lie in bed all day, then Charlotte feels they must take action. She'd saved a little money. They could start their own school, just she and Emily and Anne. What did her sisters think of that.

Anne answers enthusiastically, yes.

But they can't stray too far from home ever again. Their father has become far too sickly. He needs them, all of them there by his side. He needs them to watch over him. Charlotte will make sure their father is attended to properly.

*

Love was a thing to keep covered up.

Branwell draws himself in bed, the sheets drawn up between his legs, his head turned to the side, his hand reaching across his chest, his hand touching the tip of his right breast. His other hand reaches down again to the sheets. His heart is under there.

It is still in there in his head, the vision, even when he closes the book.

He was dreaming, dreaming only, when he shut his eyes and waited for Maria to come and touch him, to reassure him, to come and kiss him goodnight, come and take him back. If there was anything he wanted, all a boy had to do was ask in his sleep, and the dreams would surely come.

They'd link arms while walking, walking around the grounds, walking like that even up in into the hall, he and the boy playing at being Maria. They'd take turns. He'd told the boy there was nothing above them but what they dreamed they needed to heal them. He called this Maria, not God. He couldn't tell Edmund what love was, because the love felt in Angria was a stranger love. Sometimes it could even happen between a master and a child.

Charlotte knows. Charlotte knows what it feels like to be in love. She had been waiting for detailed accounts of how her brother was getting on with his pupil, the boy with a sweet temper. But her brother had stopped writing.

The boy, he mumbles to Emily, was going to go away for some time with his parents to the seaside, but then he was going to come back, so Branwell could marry his mother.

He goes on like this, dreaming aloud while Emily attends to him.

He wants to believe he'll be going back to Thorp Green.

But he's delusional. And when Young Edmund's mother marries again, she'll be sure it's to a man with a title.

*

Even when Branwell tried to draw Lydia, there was something about her that looked only like his mother.

Any further affection must be displaced.

Their only son.

Young nerves should not be shaken so.

His mind drifts off towards the clouds on the ceiling stable of the room, his movements he tries to make swim there, faces he tries to make appear, holding himself in his hand.

From the hall, one of his sisters he couldn't make out looked in at him, their brother who'd finally snapped, drowning in his poems of miseries. He'd never be able to get away from their voice in the hall, calling out to him, underneath everything, all he could have been.

He'd accidentally called the boy Maria. The boy hadn't minded. He could tell by the way the boy had held it out to him that he wanted him to take his arm.

He was to be groomed like the studs. All that stood before him was all those men there only to bring him his horse.

His mother calls them Irish. It's whispered to Young Edmund. That's how she distinguished herself from them, one of the ways.

Let him show Edmund how to hold a man down on the hay, to then be up above him, his form still so unmolded by life, by men and their fights. The men in the stables often drank and let themselves go as men must be able to do. Young Edmund had stood there before them all, one drunken night, his nature held in by the walls, swallowing and dumbfounded.

He wanted to know what they were talking about, wanted it all explained to him.

But he was to be kept sheltered.

What would his mother say, if she knew he was out there like that.

There's someone who sees everything they do.

He knew he was not supposed to be in there. His parents are too afraid to get too close to the likes of those who work for them, to see what might happen in the stables at night. He'd taken the boy's arm, to take him back out of there. It was as if the boy's body had folded up into his then, backing up into his, putting his face up against his chest. He'd once pressed against his mother in such a way. Young Edmund had buried his face there in Branwell's leg, yelling.

He'd wanted something more.

Their brother tells Emily he wants to lie on the ground, not on the bed, on the straw she must imagine with him.

Help him down.

Emily, he says. The straw still holds an imprint, can't she see that.

There would inevitably be a fictive aura to everything he said, when he wrote of the affair to his friends in letters. He was living a romance for them in his head. Those who knew him, really knew him, believed if any advances had been made towards the boy, he would have only shrunk from them.

He had to convince them.

They might see he's been lying about many things, concerning the wife.

John Brown wants the details of the whole affair. How could Branwell not oblige him, having been with this great Lady. Write letters to John Brown, tell John Brown all about it, the way it happened. She'd been like a flower, all good things, purity herself. The men he writes to, they must feel it, too. What were the words they used with each other. John Brown wants more details.

Branwell writes to his friend Grundy at the railroad, afraid Grundy might burn the letter, once he recognizes the handwriting, Branwell Brontë, with that scrawl more and more illegible towards the end of his life.

She'd fallen ill, his Lydia, from a lack of attention.

He'd given his word, to return to her. You see, she'd been mistreated, neglected by her lawful husband.

He'd been a tutor to the great Lady's son, a boy still in his whelphood. The Robinson bloodline ran deep, far back. He'd been so much better there than on the railroad, so well provided for. How kind the boy's mother had been. She'd been practically like a second mother to him. He'd been so pampered. Now he was not allowed back on any grounds.

It was love, and that's what he'd call it until his very end.

How quickly these declarations might be repeated to the wrong person.

It was rare, a woman of such sweet temper. How could he not have been tempted.

If it's beginning to sound like a romance, it was. They should all know that.

She'd remarry one day.

But it won't be Branwell.

After all, what did he have to offer such a Lady.

His troubled pleasure, soon chastised by fear.

What if they had gotten caught.

Sometimes he would accompany one or two of the horse grooms into town.

Or the new gardener, a man who might know a thing or two about where to plant the wild Irish rose.

That new gardener wouldn't work for them for too long. He didn't live there on the grounds.

He'd often have to go sleep it off in the stables.

But Branwell's charge would be there bright and early.

Branwell keeps trying to convince himself. If he found just the right words, say, in a poem, the love might be made into more, might ring truer.

If anyone could see the way Charlotte treated him now. She's not married yet.

Only Emily seems to understand, his desire to wait out for this one thing. There can be potential in such vigilance. Emily is putting on the deep blue cape she wraps around her when she goes out. Does he want to come with her.

*

The way Branwell paints Emily, one won't be able to follow her gaze, across the canvas, the remaining field, to see what she must have seen before her clearly, eyes open acceptingly.

Emily wears a dress off her shoulder.

He can catch Emily in a way he can catch no one else.

Emily, she's always thinking with her head turned in profile.

She's pretty in her silent way, blue eyes already graying at this early age. Her way is mild and introspective with all in the house. The two of them remember a day between them, how once as a child, Emily had gone into a rage over trying to keep the carpet clean, having to clean the carpet again, and she'd held a knife from the kitchen to her own throat. It was Branwell who'd calmed her, wrapping her in her blue cloak, a bit more violet then, more red, so she wouldn't hurt herself. Then she'd gone up the stairs to sleep off her fit.

Such things presaged a different temperament.

She'd once been bitten by a wild dog out on the moors, in the days before her Keeper, and fearing rabies, she'd run home, had taken the fire iron, cauterizing her own wound. It's a story everyone in Haworth knew by now.

He'd been bitten once, too, and he'd never be able to treat his own wounds the way she did.

It's tempting, as he lies there in his haze, the wind outside rapping an old oak's branches against the panes, to have Emily recall for him how she'd climbed out once, from one of the windows with no dressings, in a game, out into one of the branches that hung up alongside the house, before snapping out from under her.

So their father would not see where the missing limb should have been, she'd tried to hide the exposed underside, blackening the area with soot from the fire gone cold.

Some nights, if he has an appetite, Emily will take her dinner with him, just she and Branwell secreted off where they all used to act out their plays and write their books, the tiny bedroom.

There's the sound of Branwell, coming back home, back up the stairs, now that he's begun going out again. His shoe heels clicking softly up. He would be pleased to see her, if Emily would be there to talk to him. They'd whisper in the dark, to keep the sound down, like two children hidden together. He'll tell her more, anything she asks, about his love at Thorp Green.

Some nights they can hear Charlotte, raging silently, just the toc-toc of heels in the other room. Charlotte has begun writing a book, too, like they all always have. She was still trying to write herself a man. Her character, unlike her brother, would rise above his station. She writes about such a handsome man, a Mr. Crimsworth with his whip.

At night she eats from the hand of a man on the page, nourishing this stature. She grooms him more to be what she wants him to be. He's the love in her life now.

Anne would understand her lament. She can't believe Emily would still welcome Branwell with open arms, alone with him in the room so small, an old cupboard closet, a bed barely fitting inside. He must miss being with Charlotte, just a bit. But they won't talk about that. They'll talk about Emily's Gondals, share them among themselves as they once did.

They'll each bring one to life.

Their brother has money again, somehow, to go out drinking, to go for what he looks for in bars, taverns, pubs. Charlotte tells him again he's hopeless. And then there is his opium, never hard to get. Not at all. Cheaper than gin, certainly, though one day the unpaid bills are bound to arrive for their father to pay. How would this son ever take care of them all.

He won't. Yet he and Emily, tenderly, still loved each other like children.

What are they doing downstairs, Anne and Charlotte, who seem to stay up all hours. To get up and down the stairs, he must pass them. He has a letter in his pocket he will reach his hand in to touch periodically. Then he'll just hold his hand in there with it.

Has there been any news from Thorp Green.

There are people he writes to, but too disappointed, too angry, most of them have long since stopped replying.

Charlotte believes he's responsible in part for their father's increased blindness. But Emily won't hear of it. Charlotte would like to know why now they seem so wondrously fond of each other. They'll say nothing, though, mention nothing of how she's still writing in secret, Emily. She writes more with Branwell than she writes with them.

She should beware of being with him too much, getting too close to him.

*

Charlotte has been looking through the drawers one day in Emily's room, and found some of the poems Emily has been writing. Charlotte has now decided. They will publish their poems, the three sisters. Emily is one of them.

Emily doesn't think they should be published, can't believe Charlotte has been in her things. But Charlotte, the voice of experience, speaks. Emily, these are not common effusions! They are not at all like the poems women normally write.

Give Charlotte long enough, and she'll be able to convince you of anything. They might pay for their own book to be published. Should nobody else want to publish the poems. They have money left to them from their Aunt Branwell, whom none of them had ever really cared all that much for anyway, aside from Branwell.

For hours, days, Charlotte would try to convince Emily. Surely Emily wanted to be known. Emily should follow Anne's example. Anne was going to let her poems be published.

Yes, Charlotte thought Anne's poems were good, too. They were sweet, sincere. They'd all use the names of men. They'd done so as children, in all of their tales, all those poems then, those stories, histories. Why change that now.

And so, just as they'd once each picked their Island, they'd now each pick a Christian name.

Except Branwell, who even as a child had picked the solitary Island of Man.

Leave him to such inclinations then.

Charlotte thinks she can speak for them all when she now says we.

They'd call themselves the Bells.

Just think. The world would know them only as three brothers, Charlotte says.

They must write through the suffering.

What Branwell had been up to out there at Thorp Green had become the most common knowledge. How much clearer could Charlotte make it that she had dismissed him.

How much more vulgarly. Vulgarity perhaps he'd better understand.

Look how he blushed, when you simply mentioned Thorp Green.

But he's still their brother, Emily believes.

He went crimson.

He wouldn't ever be able to keep anything secret, Charlotte says, and what they are writing about, how they are all writing, must be kept secret. She's going to write about her teacher, M. Heger, the Master. Though Emily knows Charlotte's using other things, just as they all used to, from her own writing and Branwell's writing. They've always shared among themselves like this.

They all have to stay together now, Charlotte says, the

three sisters that they were. This is a labor to undertake very seriously, singularly focused, as the family of three brothers. It's the only way, she's sure, to cure sorrow. They'll have to be able to provide for their father.

In the dining room with her desk in front of her, Anne is engaged in finishing up the writing of Agnes Grey. After feeding, walking her dog, Keeper, Emily goes up the stairs to her bedroom, where she writes before everyone is fast asleep.

Charlotte sat on the hearth-rug, a board across her knees, writing by the fire, on the scraps of paper she'd make a fair copy of the next day for her finished manuscript.

Her own presence is the only one she must learn to tolerate.

Charlotte is writing The Master. Though maybe The Professor was a better title, for a character to fall in love with, she thinks, when the front door opens, and in walks Branwell, all their suffering. Sick again with drink, he goes straight to the fire to warm himself after the long walk back along the moors.

A long walk from up the lane, the Black Bull. He begins to cough, his cough a rattle ungluing his lungs. And then his chest heaves. Snow or mud or phlegm speckles the shirt front of his week suit.

Charlotte won't even look at him. She adjusts her reserve, her spine an erect column of exclamations, poised to rail against him. She has work to do. All of them do, all of his sisters.

And upstairs their father is dying.

Even from where she sits she can smell about him the Black Bull. Or tonight has he been to the White Horse.

Lion.

He's not afraid to answer back to Charlotte, but he is afraid of getting any closer, of going up to her, to ask to see what she's writing. And that's the way she wants it. He'd never be able to understand. Not him.

He's gone upstairs, to where Emily is writing and will show him something. He knocks on the door, the door to the small room. It's like there's a confessional between them. He'd hoped she'd still be there to talk to, still up.

Tonight he's been to the Old Cock.

She's waited up for him. Bent over the quiet white of page, she's waited for his interruption coming. These characters would all still be there, she's sure of it, tomorrow, and he's their brother.

*

To be a part of their family now, the Bells, you had to be able to fit yourself into Charlotte's story. In their brother, there was nothing but a morbid love of the coarse and brutal legend. His younger sisters should want to conduct themselves better than he has.

They write alongside each other, to try to outwrite each other in the other room, while something still has to be done about him. Early every morning now, back in Haworth, he set off to a bar like the Black Bull.

Red-eyed, pale, he'd show up, bright and early. Take off his hat, enter the door, bow solicitously with a good morning! Feel along in his pockets for money he'd managed to get a hold of, sit there, with a gin, until all his money's spent. He sits there, silent, waiting for someone to talk to him. He'll tell them all about a love they wouldn't believe, the love a woman had once felt for him.

Sunday mornings, while his family is off at church with their father, Branwell steals out of the house once alone. He'll try to get the druggist to let him have more opium. He says he needs it. All he had to do was look at the way he was shaking, a delirium of tremors going through him. Look at his hands.

Has not every house its trial. Charlotte asks those she writes to. She believes one day people will want to know about the Bells, to hear more of their poems. They've all been writing their novels. They've just got to keep trying, when nobody wants to read their poems.

Again, Charlotte says, Branwell isn't to know anything of this novel writing. Routine was what made a writer, and they must each get down to work, each produce a volume, and they can put them all together, the three sisters.

Branwell has stories he could tell them, that they could put in their books, stories from the bars like the Black Bull, of local feuds, of the passions of men, of families with long, twisted lines. He's seen more in Luddenden Foot, heard more there than the three of them put together.

He raves for Emily, performs for Emily, and she's delighted by him. He's been trying to get his job back on the railway, while they were preparing to publish their poems.

Everyone searches for the best place to put themselves in the house in relation to the others. In silence, they gathered around the fire. Returned home, they'd never be children again. Not after what they've seen. Branwell could ruin everything, he could disrupt everything.

From this a story might begin.

It's love, he says, that sweeps through there and upsets the peace of mind.

Emily loves only her Emperor Julius, who must be changed somewhat, if he's ever to be felt to be a real man, and not just a Count like Byron.

What if she called him Julian.

What if she called him after the landscape. They try to keep themselves composed in silence around his inevitable departure.

They'll still have to take care of each other.

Every night the clock is wound by their father, before he begins to try to make his own way up the stairs. He can barely see, and thus estimate the step up, the cliff of the cold stone above. He's always left his children to their own devices.

Night by night, he's gone a little more blind, until one day he won't even see them, just hear their voices gathered in the dark.

They're just words to him now.

Charlotte will help him up the stairs, or he could fall.

He can't see what he's doing.

How could he ever continue to address the church now. How long before they had to replace him.

It's as if their brother has come home to be buried alive.

At the Black Bull, the fireside was warm, always. He had his favorite chair. They leave it for him. That chair's been there for him some time now.

Lonely men, they walk up there. Their brother is one of those now.

Every night he must make his way back home. Outside the wind brings a certain tormenting. He is no longer their little King. It's hard to be in the house, as their father is surely soon to die. His sister Charlotte treats him roughly.

The Black Bull, the Black Bull calls him with its cool stones.

The church bells sing on.

At night, late at night, deep into it, there's the dark, fear of what might be waiting to embrace him out there, if he didn't keep his dreams reined in, if he let himself go completely.

Hell, he cannot write to his love.

He writes poems for papers in Halifax, so his love might see, might be recognized.

To Charlotte now he is only a disgrace, a vagabond, useless, and he knows it.

That's why he won't take his dinner with them now.

She hates to see Emily speaking to him with any kindness. This only begotten son should have never been believed in so. Look what it's done to him.

Just look how his trajectory might haunt them all.

Nobody has suffered as much as he has.

Charlotte will say nothing to him about the book she is writing. She won't speak to him. He's disappointed them all.

They might all pine for their individual love, but not as strongly as he.

Anne had seen the way he once was with William.

When walking the fields, the cheeks of their brother had bloomed bright. Passing along the heath-clad, brown summits, they had been possessed of an equilibrium, when they were going hunting.

He'd paint himself with the three of them, his sisters, himself holding his gun in the center.

His eyes had gotten larger, more luminous.

On the table, in front of them, how he'd placed them, an arrangement of the corpses of a number of pheasants.

He'd tried to paint himself taller, taller.

Anne knows that if ever this picture is to be taken out of their home, it will be held up to much scrutiny.

There was a time when on especially fine days they would all still gambol about, as children. He'd practically taught Anne to walk, holding her hand, as she'd tentatively stepped out the door.

She'd wanted to go along with them all.

She'd wanted to bring her brother with her to Thorp Green, their brother with all his troubles. When William was still there, a good influence on him, her brother and he had held arms, walking out the door.

Anne would rush to try to keep up with them.

Sometimes Anne's feet would hurt her, her little legs begin giving out on those walks, and was it right that her brother would then carry her, when she had been the smallest of four.

She's pulled along, as she's writing her book.

He won't recover, Branwell. He'll never come around. They weren't able to reason with him, and thus Charlotte feels he must only be endured.

He doesn't understand what it takes to succeed, not at all like Charlotte, or their father.

Charlotte has looked at him in a way he'll never forget. All he wanted was a motherly kindness. She'd looked at him like she was no longer the Charlotte he'd known in his childhood. It's like receiving a blow, like she'd a wild animal for a brother, a feeling he'd drink to try to sleep off.

It's Emily who has lit the little lamp in the window.

Just as she's finishing a sentence, he raps on the window.

*

Charlotte sees everything that goes on in the house now. He's still writing poems. She sees how similarly like his some of hers could be adapted, to be made to take on more current events, and not just the domestic dramas in Angria she's long come to specialize in.

The living suffer most. He's looking for a mind like his, in the poems of history, the wild wars of India and April showers. What more could he root his troubled pleasures in. Where do such notions of beauty originate.

He'd been placing ads in the paper. He wanted a new tutoring post, something that would take him far away, abroad, away from the parsonage.

He's already published poems, four in the Yorkshire Gazette.

He has the materials for his own respectably sized volume, he believes, and if he were only in London, he would try to publish a book of poems himself, like his sisters. He feels anything he would send from the address of the parsonage might only end up as fuel for the flames of an unkind, uninitiated printer's fire.

You had to make these connections personally.

His poems are as good as Anne's. Any fair judge will tell you that.

But Charlotte says he's hopeless. He's wasted his talents. These days he's not fit for much, she adds in a letter.

He has still been making the effort to send a poem off every now and then.

But his temper worsens, his health fails, his skin takes on

a sickly sheen, his eyes now hold the glassed look of the old soldiers.

Three times now he's asked for a job back on the railway, but they won't give him one. He was going to write a three-volume novel, if he could get back on the railroad, out of the parsonage. He said that long before his sisters started working on their volume of poems.

His would be full of the feelings humans veil through all their deceits.

He's taken off for Halifax, again, gotten it into his head it's for a business prospect. He knows how to spend a cheerful hour or two, by leaving the house, a cheerful day even. His sister Charlotte thinks he doesn't know what's going on, but he was going to write his own novel. To become a man of the world, one must write a novel. It is the most saleable object, he writes to his friends from the bars when not at home in the parsonage; those that would still receive his letters. Poems require the stretching of a man's intellect, but they fetch no price. With a novel, well, now he knew how much he could demand for one he could write, quietly singing to himself while puffing a big old fat cigar.

Yes, it was a harmless pleasure. Though he did want to strive to write something worthy of being read, he'd begun a novel about the crooked path of life, how life was the thing a man could go all wrong about.

In the Black Bull one day they'll all claim they've heard the story of his sister Emily's Wuthering Heights before, that book of Ellis Bell's, because of the things Branwell said when drunk.

They all think they know who it is. It's him, isn't it.

Charlotte says Ellis Bell is one of her sisters, even though

Emily doesn't want this, doesn't want to be known, like Charlotte, or Anne even, as an author of her own book. Who was this Ellis they've decided she should write under. He's an entity, created under a pen name.

He's not to be identified too closely with her. She is not Ellis, she says. How dare Charlotte ever say she, her sister, Emily, has written that book. How dare Charlotte tell everyone.

Charlotte doesn't understand what she means. Emily, she's being unreasonable, unclear. Charlotte doesn't understand why Emily doesn't want to be known as one of the three brothers.

Emily means Ellis Bell is not truly, only her. He could never be only her.

Charlotte doesn't understand why Emily will explain no more. She's gone off to her room, without another word to Charlotte, then off to the moors, to walk with the dog.

Emily will show Charlotte no more writing.

Emily will leave nothing more behind when she dies, not another novel, though Charlotte apologizes for telling people Ellis Bell is one of her three sisters. Ellis cares not to write another one.

Emily talks with him late into the night, in all his fever, going over his plans for his own book. Charlotte wouldn't want this. Charlotte believes she knows, thinks she knows who Ellis Bell is. She has become someone else, someone Charlotte herself hardly even knows.

Ellis would tell the world of a love that defied all their sister Charlotte's comprehension. Not to mention Anne's.

She's been collaborating with Branwell, like Charlotte and he once had between them. He and Emily have their secret bed plays now.

Emily shows him what he might do with his chapters. Her Lockwood might talk like her brother could write, a scholastic pretentiousness which would ultimately fail him, would ultimately serve him not at all in life, you just know.

Not in the manner their father had trained him.

From downstairs comes the chattering of tongues, reaching up to him. They tried to keep their voices low, so low upstairs you could only hear from time to time the culinary utensils in the kitchen being put away.

But sometimes they'd get carried away.

What did it matter if Emily talked to him. Words were brought together in the room like clay to play with, a rose the hardest thing to make.

No, Emily was a poet. A real poet, and she'd set off to work.

Charlotte had only been going through Emily's things, attempting to sort them out, only trying to decide the best path for her. Charlotte only had Emily's future in mind.

None of this will matter, Emily knows, once she isn't here.

Charlotte will take care of her sisters' books, as she'd taken care of their poems, as she'd destroyed many of Emily and Anne's earlier writings, which she believed could truly be of no use to anybody.

But hers, hers and Branwell's, all those she'd keep intact, the pages and pages they'd created.

*

It was as if he'd been dying already for three years. Still, he wants to do something for sweet William, wants to remember him somehow. Doesn't Anne. Doesn't Emily.

It must be something his sisters could all agree upon with him, a project for Branwell. He'll oversee the erecting of a memorial tablet for William Weightman. The people in the parish can donate what they will. Branwell has a friend, a sculptor, who can do it. He could use the money.

In Liverpool, Branwell had seen them coming off the ships, streaming off into hope, with bodies that already hung like worn coats draped about them, some too weak already to walk, stumbling up towards the line of warehouses along the quay, where they were to stay, if they could only reach them, and bed down for the night.

Until they had work, assignments.

How few of them would actually wake in the morning, images for the front pages of the London illustrated papers. They were dying, Emily, dying like him. They were like animals, no longer people, skins toughened hides, the hair an attempt to protect worried features. They died on ships, having been brought over to where life was finally to begin, was meant to be only better. They were children with no real names or homes.

*

The opium he procured for himself produced a waking memory. A wretched black bottle, their sister Charlotte says, has become his means of release.

What had he done today, but lie in bed.

Edges were dulled in a way that allowed feelings to swim together. With it, he wouldn't want too much. Just more of the opium, when he was awake again. Calming, on it, he doesn't want to reach out.

There's Maria, in the hall, his mother, sister, little charge, waiting to hold onto him, to pull him to her. He lives dreaming, air in his lungs, his blood streaming. One can see it in his eyes. His spirit, all sense of duty, takes leave of him when he gets like that.

Calmly, he's all emptied out. He wants to go to whomever will take his hand. As if he wants to be a shell, carapace, drained completely of all feeling he's been made to fill up with. He goes limp on the bed, after wearing himself out, tiring time, by walking up the lane, looking for he knows not what, walking for he knows not what anymore.

The poets with their busts will be around forever. Someone will preserve them.

You could make literature your life, if you played your cards right.

Men lean out of the shadows, as he persists up the hill, the way the horses go.

He's hurting nobody but himself.

He needed it for the pain, the way his head throbbed now, tearing him up. Give it to him. Who would administer it to him, if he needed one of them ever to do that for him. His hands in particular shook so much he could not seem to bring the glass up properly to his lips. He's spilling it.

And Emily would go over to him, steady it for him, her hands cupped around his.

Just hold it for him.

Even genius needed the help of religion and principles, Charlotte feels. Nobody wanted to publish her book. Emily's book and Anne's slender volume have found a publisher, but that's only two of the brothers.

She's started over, Charlotte, started from a new beginning.

She didn't know where it would take her, while taking their father for the operation on his eyes. He must have this operation, on his cataracts, to correct his vision, if he doesn't want to go completely blind. She fears he might never recover. She'd have to leave Emily and Anne alone at home with Branwell. She's going to take care of their father. She must separate herself from Branwell, his moral madness.

It's an insanity, their sister Charlotte believes, this obsession that has taken hold of him. He wants to feel something has been taken from him.

She knows she should pity him, but he's done this to all of them.

They're going to die ugly, she and her sisters, if all they have ahead of them is the watching over of him, waiting for the man he's become to emerge from the degradation he's brought upon himself. He seems intent on being stillborn.

She has to learn to be more quietly fascinated by his wasting away, to draw a lesson from it for her reader, to use his madness, his dissipation, his vanishing before her, shut-up in his bed, to teach. It's a madness she believes libidinal, carnal, a foil for a more virtuous, struggling heroine she's creating for herself in writing.

Sometimes she sees her brother as a woman, a woman mad.

Does their sister Emily see the devil behind his eyes, staring out of his face.

Her brother was going to be who he was. Charlotte must see that. Emily unlocks the door to let him in, the one who might be up at the indecent hour of his returns.

From the dining room, she guides the soaking drunk rag

of his body up the stairs to the bed, beside which they'll find him some mornings on the floor.

Only the reality of the pain itself matters.

A life is not a morality lesson.

He should sleep now.

Charlotte was waiting there with their father whom she'd taken for the operation on his eyes, waiting for him to recover, and she was beginning her new novel. Nobody wanted her Professor. There had to be more action. It was not good enough.

There was no possibility of just taking a simple walk, she writes, opening more naturally. She needs something soft, grave, true, passionate in her tone.

Her teeth hurt her, continue to hurt her, the aches others might take opium for until it gets better. People had to work in this life. Her heroine has to. She dreams of how there might be a happy ending in Brussels. If she works hard enough, might she still win the love of the Master.

What if the girl is a servant sent to him.

Not his student, but his servant.

What if he were a man more like an animal, her Master.

A man somewhat like the tom.

A wild hyena.

She wanted to believe him capable of love, such love, to be able to stand this separation. Her letters received no answers. If, like a child, she had pushed too hard, then perhaps she might be punished. She'd come so close to breaking down in tears in front of him. She hadn't been able to show him her true heart.

What if the Master pulls the child to him, whispers a great confession of how he loves her.

She'll call her heroine Jane. She's just a girl who waits for the right love.

If she just does all she should, all she could, for him, it will come to her.

Alone at night, in her room, she still hears voices she and her brother created in play between them. She can't escape them, ghosts taking on a life of their own.

Charlotte's heroine would look for a brother, a kindred spirit in marriage.

In her book she would lose a brother, and be inconsolable, over the loss of fondness for her younger brother.

At home he is their skeleton behind the curtains of his bed, the frame of his bones pushing out against the material of skin. He sketches himself in such lascivious poses. He sketches a skeleton bent over him, as he cannot die. Witness what he's done to himself, nobody but himself.

Her face went burning, as he gazed at her imperturbably from the bed. She wants to lock him up inside her, have him stop looking at her, in one of his moods where his eyes have turned like glass. He's retreated behind them to his imagination, a town he's peopled only with himself. He'd once been someone who not only Emily could love.

Now, because of him, they wouldn't be able to start their school. Charlotte had wanted to call it the Misses Brontë's Establishment. But children couldn't be around Branwell. They'd been whispering in town, down around the shops, drunken wastrel. He'd lost his ability to behave like a gentleman, the cold blue of his shifting eyes following Charlotte specifically around the parsonage, whenever he comes downstairs to recline in the parlor.

Only Emily doesn't feel the need to hide her face when their brother is looking longingly towards her.

Long ago, Emily will remind her, Charlotte had seen that nobody'd wanted to send any students to them, anyway.

*

His sheets were all stained.

The laudanum came in red-brown drops.

All he did was read in bed, all day long, Blackwood's, falling asleep as he read.

He falls asleep with his candle still burning.

He seems bent on destroying himself, their sister Charlotte says to Emily, to Anne. He's forgotten completely how to look after himself, but if he had a job, he'd only harm himself more by drinking more with the extra money.

Yet somehow he still managed to get a bit of money, for drinks and his opium solution. If any money was left lying around the house, he'd take it, to go out to drink. God only knew what he did down the lane, what he had. The police had even come to the parsonage, wanting to arrest him, for all the outstanding debts. They'd have to take him away to York, the prison there, if he doesn't pay everyone he owes around those parts. His sisters are going to have to come up with the money, if he can't. What kind of example was he setting for them, for the others, the Parson's only son, acting this way.

The police at the parsonage door. Something so petty, like not paying for drinks, yet it had gotten so out of hand. His sisters each retired to a room, gathered together a bit of their money, to pay for him this time. They'd pay for the drinks he still hasn't paid for. But Branwell can't let it happen again.

And he'd be out again tomorrow.

Charlotte tries not to meet his eyes.

The Black Bull was at the bottom of the lane. He just has to make his way down there, where he'd write to John Brown, ask him to help him, get him some more twists of opium, if he's been too ill, to get them for himself, tonight, or would be tomorrow, if he had no money left.

The druggist had his tonic. He needs his tonic to write.

Some nights it would be left up to Emily to walk down to the Black Bull, drag him away, bring him home.

He'd been much too petted throughout life, he berates them, that's the problem.

One night he goes to bed the only way he can sleep, drunk or drugged. In climbing into the bed, or in turning over, or in tossing about, he knocks over his candle. And then there's the thing their father has feared most all these years.

Branwell laughs in his sleep, finally warm.

He's caught the curtains around his bed on fire, too drunk even to know what he's done.

He dreams warmth as the candle catches the curtains, takes the Blackwood's, begins moving towards the sheets. Smoke began to rush in clouds from the crack of his door. There's no one there to save him, except for Emily. She hasn't quit writing yet, and she sees and feels the shadows brightening.

Or that's Anne coming up the stairs, and she calls to Emily, Maria, his sisters all indistinct to him now, as the flames lick dancing around the bed.

He's rolled onto the floor, his body motionless, mind feverishly awake in the deep of his body.

She runs down the stairs, worrying to disturb their father. His sisters warn each other not to say anything. There's a pail for water, some just out there in the hall, some water in the washstand. It has been placed everywhere, everywhere in precaution.

Branwell is dragged through the room to the corner, the windows must be opened.

She loves him as Charlotte used to, doesn't she.

She's torn down the bed curtains, stripped it, doused it.

Where's everyone else in the house.

Charlotte's seen, hasn't she.

He's to the point where they've had to pull him from his own bed.

The water hissed, like snakes around his bed.

Did he want to die. Is that what he wanted. Had he started the fire on purpose

Emily doesn't answer Charlotte.

The flames had not reached the damp woodwork of their house, luckily, or they'd have lost everything.

Someone must be watching over them, Anne says.

The bed's been blackened and scorched. The floor swam in water. His sheets ran drowned through it.

That night he's to sleep in Emily's bed. She places him there. She'd look in on him in the morning. His bedclothes are singed. The house smells all of smoke. Their father will find out. It couldn't be kept secret. But only his sisters know all the details.

It's near four. She slept on the horsehair sofa in the dining room.

Their father will find out, and Branwell will have to sleep in the future in his father's room in the bed with him.

His son will have to be looked after better.

There were moments of hallucination, moments of lucidity,

in the night, thoughts of how he might end it all for himself. If they don't give him money, he's told them he's going to kill himself. Up the stairs to the room where he will sleep with his father, he'll make his way, groping.

Their father wants to make sure he doesn't harm himself further. He's praying for him, and he wants his sisters to all do the same. His entire flock, his only son.

But there are the guns, his weapons, on the wall of his father's room, the master bedroom overlooking the expansive graveyard outside. The rain falls down and drowns itself into the ground. The bodies below the earth soak it up, the parched bodies thirsty, their bodies only pieces of dry parchment now, their souls blown about in the upper reaches of the wet trees, dripping black down.

The runoff from the cemetery runs down into their well.

Their father believes them sufficiently provided for with the hope of what they might get in the future, if they do right now, do what he says, what they've been taught. Then they would all get their reward.

He does his best, the poor old man, his son with him in the room all through the night. One morning only one of them would emerge from that room, Branwell warns his sisters. By the morning, it's likely one of them will be dead. He promises them.

They know about their father's horse-pistol, the fear of intruders every second of the day, as illogical as such a desire for control, impossible, might seem.

They listened in the night for the gun shot.

In the morning, Branwell stumbled down the stairs, still the only son, who some days is so rough with the doors their locks will then have to be mended.

Won't God protect them.

*

A cough, the grippe, a strain of influenza, they all meant Branwell was going into withdrawal, that his body was calling for the opium. He wants to be back in the arms of a dream he calls Maria.

He says he's waiting only for death. In death they might be together again.

He stays in their father's bed when their father visits the needy during the day. This is how their father tries to convince them of the Maker's worth, by offering his presence.

In the poems Branwell still struggles to sketch, to try still to find something to say of what he's felt, skeletons begin to appear, his corpses. They are men without flesh. There's that he can't begin to allow himself to grapple with realistically, couldn't come to terms with, doesn't have the words or way for. No men had come before him like him.

As the day declines before him, it's hard for Branwell to finish any poems, in this light. He writes the End of All. What else had he ever tried to do with his life. He had not done well enough. What he craves is only to embrace a savage face.

He was a boy who'd been born to a mother who would provide anything for him, everything. There was only one thing that wasn't allowed. He'd have to look for that somewhere else, make it somewhere else.

Branwell insisted on getting up out of his father's bed, on going down to the Black Bull to take his supper. He'd have brandy, once he got there, a night so cold. Once he got there, he'd only drink, not eat. The drinks are so warm. It's been a long time since he's had any dinner. He wants to die. He wants to, his heart's desire, as he goes out without his hat again.

He's been seen there, standing, in the middle of the road outside their house, crying as he paces.

No matter how much he drank some nights, he felt he could no longer live there.

He can't see past trying to get back to the stables of Thorp Green, feelings he's to die to surpass.

In writing he must use names, name. He prefers now to dream. More liberties might be taken there. He's come home to the parsonage, never again to leave.

They spend rough nights together in the master bedroom, their father believing his son's life still something worth saving and fighting for, something had to be done with him, in the room, in the bed, where his mother had died, calling out for him.

He'd shared a bed with him when he was just a little boy.

Branwell suffers from epilepsy or theatrics. Their father still believes he can find what's wrong with him in his dictionary of Modern Domestic Medicine, the painful convulsive fits, the nightmare. He notes how one cause is love, believed by some to be hereditary. His son says how he sees the demons, describes for his father a luminous substances that floats before his eyes. What's happened to their father's golden-haired boy, the lad who played with soldiers.

A remedy for intoxication was twelve drops of pure ammonia water added to a wine glass of milk, repeated ten minutes after the first dose; and then again in half an hour. Their father has to be there to watch over him.

Their father would have to wrestle with him, to try to keep him in the bed with him, to quiet him, to soothe him. Twenty-seven years ago his wife Maria, his only wife, she'd died like this, with him nursing her. He'd let nobody get any closer.

It was hard work that got their father where he'd brought them all. Charlotte finds it very forced work even to address their brother now. And love could survive anything but meanness. He would die in this room. And their father would follow him, that much is certain, but Charlotte doesn't know when.

Charlotte wonders but won't dare ask if their father is drinking again. He'll suffer the most from his boy's death, a scene that's sure to sicken them all. Angels and men must now weep for his fate, their father would rain out from the front of the church, voice trickling towards the end.

Their sister Charlotte wanted no one to see him like this. As long as their brother carried on like this, as long as he remained unable to abstain, she wanted no visitors to the parsonage.

He's ruined. Because of him, they'll all be. She can't let that happen, as long as she was still living, still drawing breath, as long as she could help it. She's the oldest.

Look at his eyes. They dim more opaque, the glass of them going more cold, the light out more inside.

Nothing more than a frame for opium and alcohol. Their father doesn't know what to do with him, in his bed, raving, how to save his only son. With an undertone to his voice, he will almost admit now they've lost him.

Charlotte writes how they've all but given up on their brother. He must have felt that, now that he was nothing. He'll stay that way, though something about him still touches Emily. She remembers how he used to be. His being was still there, in the next room, their father's bed. Though something in him had been fundamentally altered, his body having been made into this empty bottle, a vessel.

Dissipation, says Charlotte. He hasn't been writing without her.

He wrote letters only to get more alcohol.

He'd go walk in the rain, with his bad knee, to get his fix, his drink, his little peace, violently coughing, there for months after others, as whole years passed by.

*

One day their brother was visited by the Robinsons' groom from Thorp Green. He'd come to the Black Bull, seeking out Branwell, to talk to him. They'd disappeared together into the backroom, for about an hour, the door closed behind them.

They saw them go in there together.

Is he the same man Young Edmund knew quite well, and had become quite fond of. He'd get money from the Young Edmund.

His name was William, William Allison.

Gooch was a man he'd known on the railroad, but William Allison was one Branwell had met in the stables at Thorp Green. Branwell easily gets confused now.

But he's there before him again, like he was in the stables.

Yes, he knew William Allison. He remembers him, well. He's their stud groom. Everyone in the stables had known everything that had gone on, but at times they'd looked the other way. They'd adopted a certain tone speaking around him.

Though William's come to see Branwell, Branwell still can't return. He can't go back to live there. There's no chance of that. He can't go see any of them, ever again.

And Young Edmund had been taken away. He'd been given over to a new tutor.

Far from Branwell, the stables, and their influence. Far away.

After the stud groom left him, Branwell had stayed on at the Black Bull, in the backroom where they'd been together, back behind the door.

And then the groom had come out.

Down there he'd fallen into one of his fits, sounding for all his crying like a mare being mounted, still, a whole hour later, after the groom had finished whatever business with Branwell.

All the rumors of visible action must hide a deeper internal truth. Insanity is a luxury he can still believe in. The truth in his body will go with him, as he's torn away from the earth, Haworth, where as a child they'd all been gladly rooted.

A young boy was freed from care.

Young Edmund would never marry.

Once day he'd sell the estate of Thorp Green, and three years after the sale, Edmund, Eddie, Master Edmund Robinson, his character changing with the name he'd been given, depending on who the call issues from, will be drowned at thirty-seven, no longer so young, never married, extremely eligible.

They'll mount a plaque on the wall in the church.

There's no one to give that money.

The river he was trying to cross was flooded.

Too much petted, his family's name would end with him.

It was a boating accident.

He'd left a sum of money, in his will already, to be paid regularly once a year, for life, to William Allison, the stud groom who'd come to Haworth to see Branwell. He'll be buried in the family vault, a skeleton without the flesh, the blood, the skin, meat beneath the church, underneath the Robinson family pews.

*

There are the Masons, placed here and there, like the good doctor of the Robinsons who could help Branwell. They wouldn't want to see a fellow brother suffer, would they.

He made his way to their houses nights, spaced out along the landscape of moors and hills, valleys and lanes. The only way to control his urges would be to keep him from getting more money, but he's begged for further assistance, from any and everyone.

It makes a man a beggar, not having the right words for his feelings.

He's very good with coming up with these stories, as to how, and why, he's gotten so low, why all his sisters except for Emily are ashamed of him. Had he been set upon again by some man who'd wrestled him down to the ground, taken all his money, on the road, all the way down to the very last guinea. Was that why he was coming home again with his clothes in such a state.

Their sister Charlotte doesn't understand why he can't just talk plainly, as he attempts to go into one of his dramatic elaborations. Everything has to become an adventure. But they are no longer children. Where was this money coming from. Is he involved in blackmail.

He won't answer her, so she won't talk to him.

He has drunk himself and the entire house into debt.

If he's to be kept quiet, about certain things, these Robinsons would have to send him money.

He could use it for his twists of opium. From where, if not her, Mrs. Robinson, was it coming. They all know why she sends it. He's a good story about what happened between himself and the Lady of the house, once everyone's head was turned.

He gets money from the Robinson's doctor, but Charlotte still wants to know how, why. How did their brother know this widower exactly. A Freemason, like Branwell, he's a kind man who'd kindly help out his fellow brother. Emily has some money, still, from their aunt's will. She doesn't listen to her when Charlotte tells her not to invest it in the railroad.

He had friends in other towns, who'd also give him money, men he'd met in London, Bradford, on the railroad.

There were things every family had to learn to keep quiet.

The children of the Robinsons were always getting into their little scandals. There was something in the way they were raised from an early, formative, age. Anne wondered who they'd learned their morals from. Boys were to be taught to say slowly, calmly, what they wanted, and to keep their hands out of their pockets. They were to learn to entertain themselves as nicely as they could.

A boy was a medal his parents must forever try to polish.

*

Outside the window, there's the tombs that sink and lean in time, on a wall the names of the members of his family who've already gone to sleep there. Maria, Elizabeth, Maria, William, his aunt, his mother.

His course was set, his life laid to rest, out there among them. They'd add his name soon. John Brown would do it. Branwell had seen the graves elsewhere of men nobody knew how to identify beyond Porbre. Resurgam. All that marked them.

If given enough rope a legend might develop further from this anchoring of a simple start.

His heart, when he's out drinking, didn't feel so cold, but drinking just made him want more. He wants John to hold his hand. Here, John can hold his hand, he's dying. He'd begun to know himself only as this, like his character Percy, like his character, who was he.

He slips into and out of them growing in his head since he was a child. Percy, he writes about Percy, Percy came from such a line. Percy is writing the introduction to a poem Branwell is writing only for his friend Leyland.

He's not a character in one of his sisters' books.

Anne's Arthur Huntington, that's not her brother, not completely. He'd be more like Lord Lowborough, though he hasn't a title. And he hasn't a wife. Their brother never will, unlike Emily's Heathcliff, or Hindley. Perhaps, though, in other ways, he resembles Hindley.

There are ways he could have been like Charlotte's Rochester, or her John Reed.

His sisters write these books he's seen.

Success of his sisters would further punish him.

He's someone they can't get back, someone who couldn't get back to himself, as it might be said by a mother. A shining example of romantic self-destruction, and of all his sisters' hopes, an embodiment of the fears they each chose to see there, those sides of their characters. It occurs to him only now in these occasional flashes he will allow in, he's a version of their sister Charlotte's brother now, of that very wry-faced hermaphrodite she'd written him once as a child, he'd once seen himself as. One of their favorite words as children, fledglings. That was when he used the ties for the bed curtains to make his pirate sash.

Their ideas of him, of each other, came from books, the day-to-day an unbearable bleakness without the connection of a story.

He was their main character, had to try to be.

Once upon a time there was a foundling, a boy who didn't fit where he was placed.

He dreams over a scene again in his bed, as he pushes himself up against the wall.

Once or twice, at the end of a lesson, an arm around the boy's neck, a boy being taken under his wing.

The voices in the dark of his head call out to him, tell him that there's no place in Angria for a boy like him. He knows that, now that he's back home.

Heroes, leads, how boys become men, come from all his father's books.

He doesn't believe all those stories of his Hell, does he.

Let his father read him a passage again, his father train his dreams in the right direction.

This, this, this present, there in that house, that Hell that they'd made for him by putting it all in his mind, he's living it.

He couldn't get out.

He's not eating anymore because he's not hungry.

He's afraid now to go out at night without a knife he takes from the kitchen. Men hide in the dark, all up and down the lanes, and in the trees, under the leaves of the bushes, lying, to bring him down with them. Charlotte would tell him he has to watch out for them.

He reminds Charlotte of the girl she'd once had to shut

up, to punish in a closet when she was away as governess. She still dreams of that girl some nights, taking on his face. She still dreams of that creature getting out and coming after her.

Their sister Charlotte knows how to make morality work for her characters. They must each account only for themselves. As her audience may see, not all men were more capable than the women in the house. Still, they'd have to live in his shadow, as long as he lives.

Yes, Anne believes it is somewhat true.

Emily is upstairs in their father's room with their brother.

Words hide other words.

One word for his condition might be monomania.

He'd threatened in one of his drunken rages to cut his sisters' throats, but those were only words. Upstairs he plays holding the tip of one of the horse-pistols to his temple.

She should have never tried to help him, Anne.

And then one of his sisters will start crying.

They should have taken a horse-whip to him.

Anne holds onto the virtue of her principles. In sorrow, she had managed not to succumb to their influence.

If only their brother could have been made stronger.

He would call from their father's bed for them.

Whatever he says there in that bed, it's not to be repeated, only his last Amen.

Only the way he'd called out, that John Brown had been in there with him, John who would visit him in their father's warm bed, watch over him, while the rest of the family leaves for the church.

There's the tab that if he doesn't settle up soon he's going to have to appear in court over. Branwell has to keep them believing their father will settle up for him later. They know where to find him, always, at the parsonage.

He was the one who'd written himself into this corner. He's become a beast, like the walking dead, a thing wicked. They'll see him shattered. They'll see no end to it. They are not to talk to him about Heaven at a time like this. Anne is quiet, as Emily returns down the stairs.

Limp in the bed their brother lay there. Branwell had lost so much weight now, when he did get up, his clothes hung as if he'd put on their father's garments by mistake, his body little more than sticks, a born cross, when he held out his arms.

Consumption, that's what they'd call it, this illness finally.

Two and a half years spent at home like this, before he finally died.

Their sister Charlotte couldn't understand why he just wouldn't be sensible.

Their poor brother, with his blackness that would never be sponged off him, face permanently discolored, eyes always already this red. All his vices keep watch on his face. He's allowed himself to rot away like this.

To imagine that they would have seen him like this one day.

Charlotte resolves herself to have a clear conscience, in judgements she pronounces. He'd written nothing, not like she, Anne, or Emily.

But while he lived, they must endure him, though some nights he sounds like a harlot, and she doesn't want their father lying there beside him. The walls of the house are so thin, she can hear the threat of every one of the movements, how he shouts, his very breath, breath mixed with the air they all breathe.

They carry his disease in their bodies now, as their father tries to quiet his son ineffectively, failing him again, through yelling at night that endlessly wakes them. They become indistinguishable, the howlings of her brother and the wind and footfalls and her heart thudding. Charlotte stretches her head, to look out at him in the doorway. He's looking in at her, through the dark. She could swear it.

Then she hears his voice in another part of the house. Even as the smallest of children they'd written about those guns still hanging on their father's wall.

She'd come home from Brussels to this, come home to find her brother dishonored. This was the life he could call her back from, M. Heger. He still could. She'd left him, M. Heger. Was it now too late, for them.

She fears their story draws to an unhappy close.

One day Maria is going to knock on the door, then they'll know he's gone. Emily has brought a candle. Their father will be back from the church soon.

He won't leave the bed, says he won't come downstairs anymore. He knows what Charlotte is doing down there, while Emily lets him talk until he drifts, lowering his voice back down into his body, until it is just a shudder in his bones, a reflex reflecting in the window. If he won't write with them, she won't sit with them.

In Halifax, the Old Cock he'd frequent more often now that he believes they're wise to him at the Black Bull.

It's further from Haworth, but he can still walk to it.

He might have been more than what he believes himself now, haunted, and hunted, and raving some nights as if he were rabid, the lips white on his father's arm. It's a game now to look for Maria in the dark, the dark of the grave the room becomes before his eyes, before his father's support and supplication.

The dresses of his sisters, shoes, glide, tap, draping along the floor, trail through the house. He hears how he's the thorn in their flesh, a beaten boy on the bed, not even a man, a son, living out his purgatory now, a weed on the water, he writes, with no guiding star, made this way to suffer, greatness having deserted him, tossed here, wherever they'd have him, until a nightly appetite was spent, blotted out, lost, in what sleep drained from him.

It must be bought at any cost.

You don't know what it's like to live in that house, he'd say. From the Old Cock he'd write friends, out looking all night for what on weak knees, blurring his vision before him to try to see up the hill.

Some nights friends simply elude him.

He's given a hot brandy down at the bar, though he has no money. He'd walked all that way.

He'll tell anyone who'll listen how he's waiting, longing for death.

How can a person try to carry on every night, until morning, or until one of his fits overtakes him, and the knife up his sleeve falls out of his coat.

He'd taken up the study of epitaphs. The result of sorrow was your face cut into, your very appearance to yourself forever altered. He'd like, he's decided, not to be identified at all, not by name, when his time comes, only by some final reigning characteristic.

Branwell draws a man kneeling on a rock before a sinking ship. The only way to deal with this life was through abstraction. He thinks of it as a noose around his neck, no better than a murderer, fit to be hung, whose SIN has quenched his thirst for something else, something beyond a pale darkened within him.

A sketch accompanies another letter, himself naked, a

rope again, one more, noosed around his neck. A murderer he knows the name of, and has been following in the papers, that's him.

Just the worst is remembered now.

Drawings more accurately reflect his state of his mind than his words.

In words he still speaks of a Lady's love he can't have. He knows the things he says in letters may come to the receiver as bothersome, but perhaps the drawings they'll find at least entertaining.

As he wants to tell more, he must find someone he can continue to confide in. He must find a way he can. He draws himself bent over the table with wrists chained, draws himself chained to a stake and surrounded by flames that lick at his legs, placing all his torment in the hands of Mrs. Robinson, still.

Outside the breath of a low-lying, expiring God covers the ground, circles the parsonage in its spell.

He can't out walk the dark of these clouds.

He longs only to see the man he's able to write his problems to, tell everything to, a friend he could confess to. If any of the men he wrote to felt they needed to destroy his letters, after they'd read them, he'll leave that up to them. But if these things he said meant the slightest thing, anything, they might keep them.

He believes Byron still speaks to him, of what he'd lost in losing his youth. Byron sees the lost youth, everything before him now behind him. He, too, has seen himself become an old man too early. At twenty-eight, he will be that now until he dies, his eyes, he believes, the dead eyes of a fish.

It's a deeper sorrow than just the want of money.

He goes out to be with men. Together they share drink.

The promise of coming again is a resurgence towards the next day, the next night he'll be here.

He'll drink himself to death.

Men strangle each other in the shadows, all around him, and all he wants to do is fall to John Brown's feet again, one last time.

*

Fires burn through the night, in dark recesses where men come together to suffer themselves among themselves.

On his knees, he sketches, a being fallen, holding up hands empty and chained.

On his bed back home, he sketches the pugilists in the paper. He's only sketching now. His heart beats uneasily. He can listen to it, listing, in his chest, some nights, thumping harder, stumbling, trotting, accompanying him loudly trying to sleep.

He imagines one of the men in the bar taking him around the neck, with a dullness in his head, wrapping his fingers there, and throttling. Or he thinks of the shot from their father's gun, how the bullet would enter all at once, welcomed if he could still be there to feel it.

If he pulls his pencil across the page just right, the red nectar appears, rewarding sight. The hairs on his arm cast themselves in warm tints from the light that cracks through the glass.

He might earn his drink by drawing for it.

A fine oak was not to come out looking like a lily from a hothouse, the son a Miss Nancy, a milksop. He's not some fop.

He holds onto the twist of the sheets like someone's little white hand, as his reddish whiskers grow in more fully. He's seldom even up to shave. His lower jaw, around his lips, his chin, cheeks go chestnut. It grows in longer. His pencil makes longer lines. His hair falls down more over a sweat-soaked forehead.

The sheets come apart in his hands.

The door to his room was locked and shut. It's the largest room in the whole house. He had a chair there behind it. Could he be hiding anyone in there with him. Only Emily knows the secret knock.

He tells her how he'd once gone into her room at Thorp Green, Lydia's. Emily would not be able to believe how the mistress's bed had been held so grandly within the four wide mahogany pillars, polished so your face would light up in them. He'd chased the young boy around in there. And then, just as a joke, they'd slipped down into the red sheets of the bed. No light would reach them under there. They were in their cave. At this time of day, the sun was so high up in the sky.

The red blinds on the windows were left open in there, weren't drawn like the brown in his room.

His room kept all to itself on the edges of the grounds of Thorp Green.

The deep red carpet in the mother's master bedroom made it needless to tip-toe up to the boy to surprise him.

Her walls were the color of the inside of his mouth.

If Edmund comes over to the mirror, and opens up, he'll show him.

What were they doing in there.

He'd moved him down on the bed in a boxing move. The red covers work their way up into a mouth that opens up in a squeal, their strings of sweat and spit, the taste of salt, running, as they held each other down in play. The passion of the moment, let any boy try to instruct another in that. There are ways the animals comfort each other. His tongue in his mouth begins to curl up into snaking shapes, raising itself up, falling back, undulating. There in the bed turning over and over and around, he's been practicing trying to draw out the poison. His body becomes a puddle. He disturbs his body by touching it. He holds it in his hands. He can't fit all of himself into his hands. He bleeds from the mouth, when he gasps too much from the coughing fits. He can touch the red spots to the walls. Emily has come up to clean up after him.

He's ruined the nice, perfumed, satin handkerchief he'd tucked in his pocket at Thorp Green.

Their father at home might die any day now, leaving them all in the hands of the parish he'll no longer serve. They'll find Branwell on the road, panting to catch the breath for his next step, a villager, the parson's son, in such a state, trying to get home, unable, to go on, unable, to take, step the next, step alone. And then at the doorstep he's led up to, Branwell unable to lift his leg, at the last to cross himself over inside.

He sees a welcome death now, every night in dreams, as he faints away under the strain of the alcohol on his system. He remembers his sister hiding her face from him in her coffin. Already, at thirty, he's become an old man. At thirty-one decaying.

Each hour was getting closer. Soon he won't even be able to walk. The skin colored, like old papers that time ate away at.

Everyone in the village said there was madness in his eyes now. There was nothing honorable about Branwell to save. He'd let his hair go uncut. It floated around his face in bed. He was so gaunt, disappearing before them.

He believes he looks more now like one of the characters he used to write about. But he no longer writes. His knee hurts him, lying there. The warm blood grows colder. Over the course of a day, it gets colder and colder. There's no way he's going to be able to finish the poem he was working on, he was planning as a present for his friend Leyland the sculptor.

He has friends in London. He'd been just one among a million men. Men manufactured things there. The edges of the buildings had felt rough under his hands, as he'd trailed along them, as he'd leaned against them. The meeting corners were not yet all smoothed out.

Outside their horses wait for them to finish drinking. Inside the building, he runs his hands over the scaled designs. A bleeding spirit often delights in this here. Yes, men being men, being with men. Their brother, he couldn't just disappear into the labor force. He couldn't just become one of them.

In Haworth, their brother was a virtuoso in the bars, where inside the air is cold, damp, and heavy. It smelled deeply of all of them, leather of their heavy shoes, their puddles spilling, and sawdust there to take it all up. Their mouths open like the door, the air heavy with their breath, as over each other they mill, air virgin everywhere outside of there.

His sisters, Anne and Charlotte, off in London now, are taking care of the business of their books. It must be attended to.

*

Two days before he dies, he's still drinking in the village.

Shopkeepers, weavers, the chemist, the postmaster, the village children, they all watched him attempting to make his way down their Main Street.

Look how he walks.

And he didn't seem to be eating anymore, only drinking.

Here, he just needs a strong shoulder to lean on.

Some nights they hear his sister Emily even has to come down to collect him to bring him home to bed.

It's a chronic lung complaint, along with his heart.

Notice how his voice softens, as the frame of his body shakes.

Then hush falls over him.

In the night, a cough violently racks its way through his curtained body, rattling his chest, stomach, shoulders, a pale corpse struggling to still appear walking.

He goes one night to the village for the last time, in what appears to be a new state of calm that's taken over his mind. He insists on going out, though he's too weak to leave the bed, they believe.

Charlotte says nothing.

A drink. All he needs. He walks until his knee begins to give out, scanning the street, the spaces of the lanes, around corners, his widening field of vision, that begins to haze, to blur, then darken over completely in the strain. If someone could just meet him at the top of the hill, just the very top, and bring him a drink, he'll feel better tomorrow.

Friday night he'd gone to the village. That Saturday, all day that next day, he'd stayed in bed. That Sunday morning, while John Brown was there with him, watching over him, he began to die.

He'd done nothing great or good, he says to the sexton, in all his life, his friend grasping his hand. The reality of this sorrow takes him. Nothing either great or good.

John was there with him, while the family was at church. It had been years since their brother had been inside one. Not since William, his aunt. And then they'd all come back. He'd held onto John's hand, their brother, unwashed and unshaven.

He was a man moving through a mist who'd lost his way.

In this moment before their eyes, they wanted to see him again become that little boy they'd once adored.

Was he remembering childhood.

They had all been so much more then together.

He says he sees Maria, losing his reasoning.

They think he's losing his mind.

His limbs shake as if passing through them were some very strong internal breeze.

He sees only himself everywhere, not yet reached.

It's Maria, he says, he's thinking of, by calling out for. Maria, John, Maria.

Their son would no longer fit into one of their arms.

Emily recalls to him the skies they'd stood under, how he'd slip off his mother's lap, they'd all run together outside.

She'd still be there to hold them when they got back.

Charlotte had always remembered the hearth glowing, but she won't remember exactly who it was, playing there with their only boy, on the day Charlotte would never forget, watching from the other side of the door, Branwell with their older sister, mother. On her lap he'd tucked flowers into her hair all light was going out of, they'd collected weeds, but they won't call them that.

He's always been their father's favorite. She can't understand exactly why their father remains more drawn to his only boy, more than any of them. She can't let herself admit she thinks of it.

Still it eats away at her.

As a boy, Branwell had known about their different bodies. A woman would have the patience, he believes, for the pain he doesn't. When his father had placed him under the mask of his hands, hiding his son's face behind them, to see how smart he really was, what he speaks out from the dark behind there, when asked why men and women think differently, Branwell's answer is because of their bodies.

Then Maria had slipped behind their father's hands, so he would see she could answer, too. Prepare for a happy eternity, that's how one was to spend one's time, Maria, intelligent, replied.

Sweat stood out around Branwell's eyes, as if he was trying to turn and unlock something inside himself. He'd turned away on the bed from facing Emily, his chest racked with an internal storming that grotesquely bows him up and back.

They say she is in that place where you no longer felt the need for anything anymore, but Branwell knew she was only in all those words in their heads, words that had been there on paper once. He could feel her in the air over his bed, a stain bruising the air, hovering up to the surface, before retreating back healing. She must be unhappy wherever she's gone. She seems so often to be reaching for him.

There is a world below, Branwell. It is where you will go. It is where they will all be waiting for you.

You were a young angel, the lightness of your fingers wings feathered.

They all watched his skin becoming stiff as colored marble. The wind in the room feels just as cold their brother's hands.

And then there would be a smile on his face, if she, Emily, was to take his in hers.

His body there their brother no longer.

He goes lying down like this, and Emily of a sudden decides she wants to die standing.

*

He was to die in his father's arms, with letters in his pocket, but none from Mrs. Robinson. These letters were from a gentleman friend of his, living near Thorp Green, an acquaintance.

His body lies like marble in the other room. It must lie there as it must be prepared for burying. For days it will have to stay here.

For Sunday, Monday, Tuesday, Wednesday, Thursday.

It's such a small house, Charlotte falls ill.

*

Their brother's removal from them is called by Charlotte a thing of mercy. She could never allow herself to marry a man who resembled him. She could not spend the rest of her life with such reminders.

She'd marry instead one day their father's new curate.

When he'd begun to write again, after returning home, Branwell had written in a woman's voice of the change from girlhood to womanhood. After the body was removed, Charlotte goes into his room, to find any letters, papers, and to burn them. It's normal procedure.

He's been writing all this time in his room, in their father's bed. Things have to be controlled more. Charlotte makes a bundle of the pages. Emily, sick with what appears to be a cold, will not protest the putting them in the fire. Anne is silent. She said nothing.

Her brother, he'd left of his own accord. She, Charlotte, knew what was best for all of them. Never ask her again about Brussels.

She is soon to be a great writer, though at first under a man's name. She'd had to write like that, like one, she believed, to be taken seriously. It was not like when they'd all written together. Her Jane Eyre is rushed out. Their sister Charlotte, intent on preserving her version of all things, preserving them all, she's written a better ending.

But the gossip, gossip exists, widespread, running like moor fire gone wild, over the sweetbriar. It sounds a good story. Servants and gardeners, they are the ones you have to watch out for.

His Thorp Green Notebook has gone completely missing.

Their sister Charlotte sees to all such loose ends, as it's one of her jobs now. Language has been given to us to make our meaning perfectly clear, their sister Charlotte believes, and she doesn't understand why anyone would ever need to wrap their meaning in dishonest doubt.

Why couldn't everyone just afford to be as honest as she'd been.

She had to watch out for their future, she alone.

She knew what to keep, what might be something, what was only childhood material, letters of Emily's and Anne's, writings of theirs that could be burned, too.

*

Their sister Charlotte needed to turn her attentions to Emily now, a girl who had somehow come to such knowledge of evil as might run in men's hearts, her horrors concealed by abstractions, like the study of the root of heath. The flowers themselves might be bell-shaped, but look how to not slip off, to hold its purchase, sustain itself in the coppery brown, infertile soil, it must form underneath the ground its claw.

Somewhere else, in some other time, they might not have written at all, their sister Charlotte says.

Emily says after a certain point there was simply no hope for their brother. But she couldn't believe, purely, the picture Anne painted in her book to be like their brother. And she couldn't believe the way Charlotte had reacted. Emily, she had compassion for him, those last three months of her own life, after their brother's death. Emily wanted then to die without them feeling sorry for her either.

Bodies thought their own ways.

Bodies wanted to follow themselves.

As a child, she'd told their father that Branwell must first be reasoned with, when he was being bad, and then, when he wouldn't listen, if he wouldn't, he must be whipped.

He should have been beaten like a horse brought into line. They should have taken a firmer hand earlier with him. He'd not have drifted so far from their fold, then.

It might have taught him.

Their father'd let him get away with too much too early. Only training could supplement breeding. But then, that was the human spirit, his own, that would flash up out under the strokes, a pressure built all up inside him, that cries out, the last sound he'd made almost not even human.

What did she suppose it's like, Emily, to be buried alive in the agony of a rose. What would it spell out, if each petal were a word, if each word were held in his hand, if he could give them all to her. What would he say if he could tell her anything.

She'd told him not to worry, not to hurt his words, rest now.

They'd decorated the room with their words.

A feeling was tamed somewhat by drawing it in.

She'd watched his clear eyes gazing wistfully at his drawing Master. She'd noticed the way the boy's face tended to fright, to whiten, his eyes going wider, and then downcast, little lips curl up into a mouth, trembling, like petals drawn in, the more alone they got, out towards the shadows of the graveyard.

He'd taken him there from time to time for them to do a sketch or two. He'd told him there was nothing to be afraid of, that there were no ghosts.

Had they ever sat on their father's knee, like Branwell had sat there on their mother's lap, looking at the most appropriate books together, turning the leaves of the volume over.

They might depict the various breeds of horses in one. Their musculature, hindquarters, haunches, all pointed out, pronounced, named in all the fine detail.

*

They remember a summer in Haworth, remember Branwell stretched out under a tree, as lazily the rose-red violets picked only to feed his leaves of poetry, to mark his place in the book.

Already his sisters are just three.

They'd all thought of Maria. He'd looked like Maria dying, hair coming out in handfuls, the clothes underneath all stained wet.

Maria lived somewhere in the light around their house, like the wind and roots that grew into stone, that made dust of the old graves. Even the rocks were broken further down, by something you couldn't see. Not a single one of them remembers their mother's face. She was God. Emily, on her knees under the tree, picking at the grass, begins to bury her fingers down in the soil that will hold it, with a firm grip, now holds him.

This end has been written long ago. Where'd he gone, how would they dream him now. To dream him as a boy, a child, would it all be the same trouble starting over again, all in its infancy. To dream of a child is a curse.

Their little parsonage had become a place where death swam in the air, gathering in invisible clouds, passing from one of their mouths to another. The little cough, small appetite, the shortness of breath, they'd all been coming for years, the cold that could not be shaken, thick wind trapped in the branches of lungs.

There are many names for these diseases, like consumption, tuberculosis. Charlotte sees them all in another light now, as Emily caught her cold, her death unknowingly, at the funeral Charlotte had been too sick to go to.

When their brother died, at thirty-one, his body the body they would now try to walk around, they must only go on writing, though for days Charlotte couldn't answer her correspondence. Anne would see to Charlotte's letters for her; Anne, whom Charlotte had someone like Branwell call in a story nothing, absolutely nothing.

Once their brother had been removed from the house, the girls Anne had taught at Thorp Green would be able to come visit her at Haworth.

It was a house full of temptations, where even one of the daughters had gone to seed like the boy who couldn't be reared right.

But the ones Anne had had a good influence on would come visit her.

Charlotte did not believe in crying, simply because she was sad. Long ago she'd lost any image of Branwell she could lean on. He hadn't been her dear friend for some time. She cried only because he could have been something like all of them, the rest of them, someone she could be proud of. He'd failed miserably.

He might finally have been forgiven, called back from his straying, Anne reminds her.

Emily listened to the thunder at his funeral. Such a torrential rain would have been a joy for Branwell. She sat in the damp church, walking home across the damp of the soaked moors in only her thin shoes. When she gets sick, she'll refuse to see a doctor. Emily doesn't believe in such things, a body will do what it must.

She'll not tell Charlotte or anyone what's wrong with her.

To be in the earth, to return to the earth, that's what she thinks, Emily, consumption now galloping, comb there on the floor, something she'd dropped.

She'll go back as she came from.

Listen, now, to the wind.

*

After the death of their brother Anne's second book will go into a second edition. It will be a greater success than her first book of prose about being a governess.

She felt a bitterness towards the truth might affect its reception, that the hasty glance might judge too quickly. She'd been forced to write this because of what she'd seen. It was not an attempt to gratify her own taste, she wants to assure you.

You must know creation carries along with it its own morality. See, she was not like their brother. She was better, Charlotte might tell her, as courage was required to continue trying to create, and she was the one writing here.

We must strive for the right things, Anne believed.

By then the dust would have settled in their brother's room.

Who had made him want the things he'd believed he'd wanted.

This was not soft nonsense. This was not how everyone in the world was like everyone else in the world. Not all prose could be so polished. Nor should it be, Anne believed. The writing should be as brutal as his nature had been.

All she hoped was that she'd accomplished that, that she hadn't allowed her reader to view from too safe a distance, to take courage in the fact that such a life might only be fiction, and not the true thing to struggle with day in, day out.

Why had he believed he had to live a history, a romance, the two becoming interchangeable through their mutual influence on each other, in order to live.

Did it matter if she is a man or a woman writing with such insight.

Stories lead you into wanting experience, as if you had no store of your own. And from experience the bitter truth was wrung. The case of her character was an extreme one, she believed, in keeping with that courage. She would know such characters had once existed. If one person has been saved, her book has done its job. To safeguard innocent pleasure, unpalatable truths must first be spoken.

Their sister Charlotte would take up for her. Perhaps it was a mistake, perhaps Anne never should have written what she had, but she'd take up for her. There had to be reasons. Surely it had not come from her sister's own imagination, to ask a reader to believe someone had once hidden in the bushes, waiting for someone to join them there. Anne herself would never do such things.

Her motives were slightly morbid, and she was naturally dejected, Charlotte concedes, but what Anne had seen at Thorp Green had done her harm. A self-indulgence would have been the easy way out, to not write about the truth of her own pain, to allow her self to luxuriate in forgetfulness.

She found an ever ineffable tenderness in a dialect that held Haworth inside it. This language they used, these passions they showed, this violence they let loose, it couldn't stem only from their imaginations. Charlotte insisted it was their reality, the reality of her sisters. They'd seen it before them every day, the cruel hard facts of being made to live as they had.

Anne herself believed she'd written a good book, a necessary book, and Anne's life would be a brief, blameless one. She wanted to go to Scarborough again, one last time. Surely she could tell her sisters what had happened there, but she wouldn't. She'd tell them nothing. She wants to enjoy the rest of her time there in silence.

*

Just months after Branwell, Emily will die.

Their sister Charlotte will have to keep writing, holding onto something, her pencil.

Anne, too, had little strength left, and she'd die at twenty-nine.

They had all left Charlotte then, but for their father, but for their books, those who'd written them, her sisters.

Before she married the new curate, Charlotte had been working on a book started in pencil, another one of a Master and his charge. And then the theme of two brothers believed in many ways she and Branwell, as he'd descended to a railway clerkship, she'd gone off to Brussels, in her attempt to further her station.

But she couldn't get inside of his head, not in the way she wanted to, wanted to be able to, couldn't make him sing the way she could heroines, if she just knew she was going to in the end give them the man they'd always wanted.

All she could seem to do was rewrite the few pages she'd already written, what'd already been said, descendants of characters she's known and reworked for years, from plays of her and Branwell, when not writing letters to the new curate, Arthur.

He had a Bell in his name, too.

If it weren't for her marriage, she'd have been writing right then. And Arthur would be the one to tell her she couldn't keep repeating herself, with all these schools she always seemed to begin with, though once she'd started along those lines, she said, she could always change it later. She just needed the school to start.

Her brother had just needed the world.

But there's little time for thinking, Charlotte says, when you had a husband. A husband was not like a brother, not at all. You had to be faithful to him until the very end.

We all seek an ideal life, Charlotte wrote. No longer a young girl, God's bride, she wrote of a charge taken into the arms of someone much stronger, told to have no fear, to go ahead, that it was all right, lay its little head calmly against the stronger one's largeness, gradually let the meaning of their joining become a reassurance.

Was this a love he'd desired. They'd prayed for him, prayed for the boy.

They were only happy with Branwell when he'd tried to please them.

The only feelings they'd keep were the ones they wanted him to feel.

He didn't dare hope for forgiveness, as fate became an increasingly darkening thing, didn't dare ask.

Their sister Charlotte will die in labor, less than a year after she'd married the curate who'd delivered the memorial address of her brother.

Only then would their father follow.

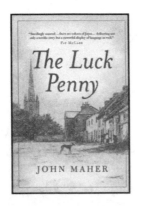

JOHN MAHER
The Luck Penny

A compelling story of life and death, of loss and trauma; a story, too, of colonisers and natives, of language and power.

"There are echoes of Joyce, delivering not only a terrific story but a powerful display of language as well. There are resonances of Ackroyd and Stevenson, and the feel for London and the past never errs. This is a novel where place really matters — authenticity seeps from the page, whether teeming municipality or quiet Irish midlands village in a far-flung corner of the hegemonic British Empire in 1849."
Pat McCabe

ISBN 978-0-86322-361-7; paperback original

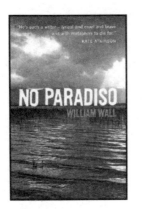

WILLIAM WALL
No Paradiso

Evocative, haunting short fiction by 2005 Booker longlisted author William Wall

The stories in this outstanding collection range in location between Ireland, Italy and the USA. Varying in structure, they explore themes of loss, love and language. Many are haunting and evocative, some are mischievous or slightly surreal, some brutally dark.

"William Wall is a genuine literary talent, with a poet's gift for apposite, wry observation, dialogue and character... [He] has an admirable power of poignant description." *Guardian*

ISBN 978-0-86322-355-6; paperback original

EMER MARTIN
Baby Zero

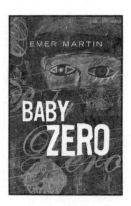

"An incendiary, thought-provoking novel, like a haunting and spiritual ballad, it moves us and makes us care." Irvine Welsh

A darkly comic novel, *Baby Zero* is set in California, Ireland and an unheard of country, where each successive Taliban-like regime turns the year back to zero, as if to begin history again. A woman, Marguerite, imprisoned for fighting the fundamentalist government, is pregnant. To retain her sanity she tells her unborn child the story of three baby zeros – all girls from a family that has been scattered across the globe, all born at times of upheaval. Despite its unflinching portrayal of extreme oppression, *Baby Zero* constantly bubbles with humorous incident and characters, presenting a compelling and entertaining satire on both east and west.

ISBN 978-0-86322-355-6; paperback original

MARY ROSE CALLAGHAN
Billy, Come Home

"At the heart of this innocent-seeming novel lies a scathing critique of attitudes to mental illness. Mary Rose Callaghan's velvet-gloved hand wields a pen as sharp as a razor. An honest look at how we really are, this is not a novel to forget in a hurry." Éilís Ní Dhuibhne, Orange Prize shortlisted novelist

Billy, Come Home is a compelling, dramatic story of schizophrenia, murder and the rush to judgement; a story of prejudice and consequent tragedy. A thirty-year old woman travels to London to identify a body that has been fished out of the Thames; it is believed to be that of her brother, Billy. The narrative flashes back to the brutal murder of a teenage girl when Billy is regarded suspiciously by the neighbours, one of whom sends poison pen letters, setting a train of events in motion.

ISBN 978-086322-366-2; paperback original

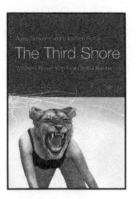

**AGATA SCHWARTZ AND
LUISE VON FLOTOW (EDS)**
The Third Shore
Women's Fiction from East Central Europe

A rich compendium of fiction by twenty-five women from eighteen nations, *The Third Shore* brings to light a whole spectrum of women's literary accomplishment and experience.

The Third Shore brings to light a whole spectrum of women's literary accomplishment and experience virtually unknown in the West. Gracefully translated, and with an introduction that establishes their political, historical, and literary context, these stories written in the decade after the fall of the Iron Curtain are tales of the familiar reconceived and turned into something altogether new by the distinctive experience they reflect.

ISBN 978-0-86322-362-4; paperback original

DRAGO JANČAR
Joyce's Pupil

"Jančar writes powerful, complex stories with an unostentatious assurance, and has a gravity which makes the tricks of more self-consciously modern writers look cheap [...] Drago Jančar deserves the wider readership that these translations should gain him." Micha Lazarus, *TLS*

ISBN 978-0-86322-340-2; paperback original

NENAD VELIČKOVIĆ
Lodgers

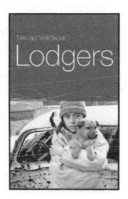

"Nenad Veličković offers a beautifully constructed account of the ridiculous nature of the Balkans conflict, and war in general, which even in moments of pure gallows humour retains a heartwarming affection for the individuals trying to survive in such horrific circumstances." Siobhan Murphy, *Metro*

ISBN 978-0-86322-348-8; paperback original

KATE McCAFFERTY
Testimony of an Irish Slave Girl

"McCafferty's haunting novel chronicles an overlooked chapter in the annals of human slavery . . . A meticulously researched piece of historical fiction that will keep readers both horrified and mesmerized." *Booklist*

"Thousands of Irish men, women and children were sold into slavery to work in the sugar-cane fields of Barbados in the 17th century . . . McCafferty has researched her theme well and, through Cot, shows us the terrible indignities and suffering endured." *Irish Independent*

ISBN 978-0-86322-338-9; paperback original

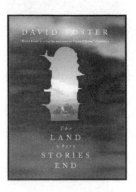

DAVID FOSTER
The Land Where Stories End

"Australia's most original and important living novelist." *Independent Monthly*

"A post-modern fable set in the dark ages of Ireland. . . [A] beautifully written humorous myth that is entirely original. The simplicity of language is perfectly complementary to the wry, occasionally laugh-out-loud humour and the captivating tale." *Irish World*

"I was taken by surprise and carried easily along by the amazing story and by the punchy clarity of the writing. . . This book is imaginative and fantastic. . . It is truly amazing." *Books Ireland*

ISBN 978-0-86322-311-2; hardback

CHET RAYMO
Valentine

"Such nebulous accounts [as we have] have been just waiting for someone to make a work of historical fiction out of them. American novelist and physicist Raymo has duly obliged with his recently published *Valentine: A Love Story.*" *The Scotsman*

"[A] vivid and lively account of how Valentine's life may have unfolded… Raymo has produced an imaginative and enjoyable read, sprinkled with plenty of food for philosophical thought." *Sunday Tribune*

ISBN 978-0-86322-327-3; paperback original

BRYAN MACMAHON
Hero Town

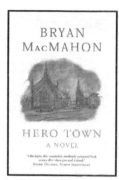

"*Hero Town* is the perfect retrospective: here the town is the hero, a character of epic and comic proportions. . . It may come to be recognized as MacMahon's masterpiece." Professor Bernard O'Donohue

"For the course of a calendar year, Peter Mulrooney, the musing pedagogue, saunters through the streets and the people, looking at things and leaving them so. They talk to him; he listens, and in his ears we hear the authentic voice of local Ireland, all its tics and phrases and catchcalls. Like Joyce, this wonderful, excellently structured book comes alive when you read it aloud." Frank Delaney, *Sunday Independent*

ISBN 978-0-86322-342-6; paperback original

JOHN B. KEANE
The Bodhran Makers

The first and best novel from one of Ireland's best-loved writers, a moving and telling portrayal of a rural community in the '50s, a poverty-stricken people who never lost their dignity.

"Furious, raging, passionate and very, very funny." *Boston Globe*

"This powerful and poignant novel provides John B. Keane with a passport to the highest levels of Irish literature." *Irish Press*

"Sly, funny, heart-rending. . . Keane writes lyrically; recommended." *Library Journal*

ISBN 978-0-86322-300-6; paperback

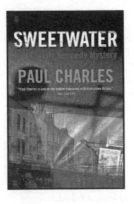

PAUL CHARLES
Sweetwater
A DI Christy Kennedy Mystery

Christy Kennedy is an Ulsterman living in leafy Primrose Hill and working in vibrant Camden Town. He loves the art of detection, he's addicted to the puzzle of the crime.

"Paul Charles is one of the hidden treasures of British crime fiction." John Connolly.

"Agatha Christie for people who inhale." Nigel Williamson *The Times*

ISBN 978-0-86322-356-3; hardback

JACK BARRY
Miss Katie Regrets

From the criminal underbelly of Celtic Tiger Dublin comes a gripping story of guns, drugs, prostitution and corruption.

A seemingly humdrum shooting leads a detective to an online male prostitution service and to hints of a link with a corrupt politician.

"A startling, powerfully entertaining thriller... [with] a tremendous sense of modern Dublin... For my money, this author is one of this country's finest talents." Pat McCabe

ISBN 978-0-86322-354-9; paperback original

SAM MILLAR
The Darkness of Bones

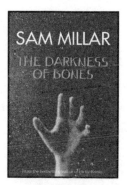

A tense tale of murder, betrayal, sexual abuse and revenge, and the corruption at the heart of the respectable establishment

A young boy discovers a bone in a snow-covered forest. Initially, he thinks it could simply be that of an animal. But it belongs to a young girl who has been missing for three years. Meanwhile, in a derelict orphanage, a tramp discovers the sexually mutilated and decapitated corpse of its former head warden.

ISBN 978-0-86322-350-1; paperback original

KEN BRUEN (ED)
Dublin Noir

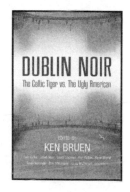

Nineteen previously unpublished stories by acclaimed crime writers, each one set in Dublin

Brand new stories by Ray Banks, James O. Born, Ken Bruen, Reed Farrell Coleman, Eoin Colfer, Jim Fusilli, Patrick J. Lambe, Laura Lippman, Craig McDonald, Pat Mullan, Gary Phillips, John Rickards, Peter Spiegelman, Jason Starr, Olen Steinhauer, Charlie Stella, Duane Swierczynski, Sarah Weinman and Kevin Wignall.

ISBN 978-0-86322-353-2; paperback original

KEN BRUEN
WINNER OF THE SHAMUS AWARD FOR BEST NOVEL, FINALIST FOR THE EDGAR, BARRY AND MACAVITY AWARDS

The Guards

"Bleak, amoral and disturbing, *The Guards* breaks new ground in the Irish thriller genre, replacing furious fantasy action with acute observation of human frailty." *Irish Independent*

"With Jack Taylor, Bruen has created a true original." *Sunday Tribune*

ISBN 978-0-86322-323-0; paperback

The Killing of the Tinkers

"Jack Taylor is back in town, weighed down with wisecracks and cocaine ... Somebody is murdering young male travellers and Taylor, with his reputation as an outsider, is the man they want to get to the root of things ...Compulsive ... rapid fire ... entertaining." *Sunday Tribune*

ISBN 978-0-86322-294-8; paperback

The Magdalen Martyrs

"Exhibits Ken Bruen's all-encompassing ability to depict the underbelly of the criminal world and still imbue it with a torrid fascination... carrying an adrenalin charge for those who like their thrillers rough, tough, mean and dirty." *The Irish Times*

ISBN 978-0-86322-302-0; paperback

The Dramatist

"Collectively, the Jack Taylor novels are Bruen's masterwork, and *The Dramatist* is the darkest and most profound installment of the series to date... Readers who dare the journey will be days shaking this most haunting book out of their heads." *This Week*

ISBN 978-0-86322-319-8; paperback original